꺼삐딴 리

아시아에서는 《바이링궐 에디션 한국 대표 소설》을 기획하여 한국의 우수한 문학을 주제별로 엄선해 국내외 독자들에게 소개합니다. 이 기획은 국내외 우수한 번역가들이 참여하여 원작의 품격을 최대한 살렸습니다. 문학을 통해 아시아의 정체성과 가치를 살피는 데 주력해 온 아시아는 한국인의 삶을 넓고 깊게 이해하는 데 이 기획이 기여하기를 기대합니다.

Asia Publishers presents some of the very best modern Korean literature to readers worldwide through its new Korean literature series 〈Bilingual Edition Modern Korean Literature〉. We are proud and happy to offer it in the most authoritative translation by renowned translators of Korean literature. We hope that this series helps to build solid bridges between citizens of the world and Koreans through a rich in-depth understanding of Korea.

바이링궐 에디션 한국 대표 소설 **105**

Bi-lingual Edition Modern Korean Literature 105

Kapitan Ri

전광용
꺼삐딴 리

Chŏn Kwangyong

ASIA
PUBLISHERS

Contents

꺼삐딴 리

Kapitan Ri

수술실에서 나온 이인국(李仁國) 박사는 응접실 소파에 파묻히듯이 깊숙이 기대어 앉았다.

그는 백금 무테안경을 벗어 들고 이마의 땀을 닦았다. 등골에 축축이 밴 땀이 잦아들어감에 따라 피로가 스며 왔다. 두 시간 이십 분의 집도(執刀). 위장 속의 균종(菌腫) 적출. 환자는 아직 혼수상태에서 깨지 못하고 있다.

수술을 끝낸 찰나 스쳐가는 육감, 그것은 성공 여부의 적중률을 암시하는 계시 같은 것이다. 그러나 오늘은 웬일인지 뒷맛이 꺼림칙하다.

그는 항생질(抗生質) 의약품이 그다지 발달되지 않았던 일제시대부터 개복 수술에 최단 시간의 기록을 세웠

Yi Inguk, M.D., emerged from the operating room and buried himself deep in the reception room sofa.

Dr. Yi lifted his platinum rimless glasses and mopped his forehead. As the sweat on his back dried, fatigue began to sink into his body. Two hours and twenty minutes in surgery, removing an abdominal abscess. The patient had not yet recovered consciousness.

He would feel a presentiment the moment an operation was over, a revelation of the chances of success. But today, for some reason, he came out of it feeling leery.

던 것을 회상해 본다.

맹장염이나 포경(包莖) 수술, 그 정도의 것은 약과다. 젊은 의사들에게 맡겨버리면 그만이다. 대수술의 경우에는 그렇게 방임할 수만은 없다. 환자 측에서도 대개 원장의 직접 집도를 조건부로 입원시킨다. 그는 그것을 자랑으로 삼아왔고 스스로 집도하는 쾌감마저 느꼈었다.

그의 병원 부근은 거의 한 집 건너 병원이랄 수 있을 정도로 밀집한 지대다. 이름 없는 신설병원 같은 것은 숫제 비 장날 시골 전방처럼 한산한 속에 찾아오는 손님을 기다리고 있는 형편이다.

그러나 이인국 박사는 일류 대학병원에서까지 손을 쓰지 못하여 밀려오는 급환자들 틈에 끼여 환자의 감별에는 각별한 신경을 쓰고 있다.

그것은 마치 여관 보이가 현관으로 들어서는 손님의 옷차림을 훑어보고 그 등급에 맞는 방을 순간적으로 결정하거나 즉석에서 서슴지 않고 거절하는 경우와 흡사한 것이라고나 할까.

이인국 박사의 병원은 두 가지의 전통적인 특징을 가지고 있다.

He recalled the time he had set a record for the shortest abdominal operation since Japanese colonial days, when antibiotics weren't so advanced.

Appendicitis or circumcision—such surgery is a simple matter. It can be turned over to the young doctors and forgotten. But one cannot be so casual about major surgery. The patients feel that way, too. Most allow themselves to be hospitalized on the condition that the director himself operate. For Yi Inguk, M.D., this was a matter of pride, and he felt a real sense of pleasure in wielding the knife.

His clinic was in a neighborhood so busy and crowded that it seemed nearly every second building was another clinic or hospital. But this nameless modern facility actually waited in empty leisure for its clients, like a country shop between market days.

When he received his clientele—the overflow emergency cases passed on to him by a busy, first-rate university hospital—Yi Inguk, M.D., would take his time, exercising as much concern as each patient's appearance recommended. He was perhaps like an innkeeper who takes one look at a new arrival's clothing and instantly decides which room to give him or unhesitatingly turns him away without

병원 안이 먼지 하나도 없이 정결하다는 것과 치료비가 여느 병원의 갑절이나 비싸다는 점이다.

그는 새로 온 환자의 초진(初診)에서는 병에 앞서 우선 그 부담 능력을 감정하는 데서부터 시작한다. 신통치 않다고 느껴지는 경우에는 무슨 핑계를 대든 그것도 자기가 직접 나서는 것이 아니라 간호원더러 따돌리게 하는 것이다.

그렇게 중환자가 아닌 한 대부분의 경우 예진(豫診)은 젊은 의사들이 했다. 원장은 다만 기록된 진찰 카드에 따라 환자의 증세에 아울러 경제 정도를 판정하는 최종 진단을 내리면 된다.

상대가 지기[1]나 거물급이 아닌 한 외상이라는 명목은 붙을 수 없었다. 설령 있다 해도 이 양면 진단은 한 푼의 미수나 결손도 없게 한 그의 반생을 통한 의술 생활의 신조요 비결이었다.

그러기에 그의 고객은 왜정시대는 주로 일본인이었고 현재는 권력층이 아니면 재벌의 셈속에 드는 측들이어야만 했다.

그의 일과는 아침에 진찰실에 나오자 손가락 끝으로 창틀이나 탁자 위를 훑어 무테안경 속 움푹한 눈으로

stirring from his seat.

The clinic of Yi Inguk, M.D., had two characteristics. The interior was kept spotless, and the fees were at least twice as high as at any other place. His examination of a new patient began with an inquiry into his ability to pay, followed by questions about his disease. If the patient didn't seem such a good prospect, the doctor would offer some excuse. Not personally, of course—his nurse would show the person out.

In all but the most serious cases, younger doctors conducted the preliminary examination. The Director then had only to make a final diagnosis—based on a judgment of the patient's physical condition and economic status, which had been duly recorded on the examination card.

Except for very close friends and the socially prominent, there was no such thing as credit here. Even admitting the little credit given, his twofold diagnosis was the secret of his practice, the guiding principle of thirty-some years of medical life that had seen neither penny lost nor penny uncollected. Hence, his clientele had been mainly Japanese during the occupation and now had to be among the ruling political circles or the great business mag-

응시하는 일에서 출발한다.

이때 손가락 끝에 먼지만 묻으면 불호령이 터지고, 간호원은 하루 종일 원장의 신경질에 부대껴야만 한다.

아무튼 단골 고객들은 그의 정결한 결백성에 감탄과 경의를 표해 마지않는다.

1·4 후퇴 시 청진기가 든 손가방 하나를 들고 월남한 이인국 박사다. 그는 수복되자 재빨리 셋방 하나를 얻어 병원을 차렸다. 그러나 이제는 평당 오십만 환을 호가하는 도심지에 타일을 바른 이층 양옥을 소유하게 되었다. 그는 자기 전문의 외과 외에 내과, 소아과, 산부인과 등 개인병원을 집결시켰다. 운영은 각자의 호주머니 셈속이었지만 종합병원의 원장 자리는 의젓이 자기가 차지하고 있다.

이인국 박사는 양복조끼 호주머니에서 십팔금 회중시계를 꺼내어 시간을 보았다.

2시 40분!

미국 대사관 브라운 씨와의 약속 시간은 이십 분밖에 남지 않았다. 이 시계에도 몇 가닥의 유서 깊은 이야기가 숨어 있다. 이인국 박사는 시계를 볼 때마다 참말 '기

nates to qualify at his door.

His daily routine began with an appearance in the examination room, where his first act was to draw his fingertips along the window frames or table tops and peer, with sunken eyes through rimless glasses, at what he had found. If this inspection revealed any dust he erupted in a thunderous rage, and the nurses faced another day of bad temper from the Director. His regular clientele, however, were full of admiration and respect for such spotless integrity.

This was Yi Inguk, M.D., who had fled to southern Korea during the January Retreat in 1951, carrying only his black bag with a stethoscope in it. Then, as soon as Seoul was recovered, he had quickly rented a room that he outfitted as a clinic. But now he had a two-story Western-style building in downtown Seoul where land was extremely expensive. In addition to his own specialty, surgery, this private hospital also offered departments of internal medicine, pediatrics, obstetrics, and so on. While the profit and loss of each department was its own concern, the directorship of the general hospital resided in his dignified person.

적'임에 틀림없었던 사태를 연상하게 된다.

왕진 가방과 함께 38선을 넘어온 피란 유물의 하나인 시계. 가방은 미군 의사에게서 얻은 새것으로 갈아 매어 흔적도 없게 된 지금, 시계는 목숨을 걸고 삶의 도피행을 같이한 유일품이요, 어찌 보면 인생의 반려이기도 한 것이다.

밤에 잘 때에도 그는 시계를 머리맡에 풀어 놓거나 호주머니에 넣은 채로 버려두지 않는다. 반드시 풀어서 등기서류, 저금통장 등이 들어 있는 비상용 캐비닛 속에 넣고야 잠자리에 드는 것이었다. 거기에는 또 그럴 만한 연유가 있었다. 이 시계는 제국대학을 졸업할 때 받은 영예로운 수상품이다. 뒤쪽에는 자기 이름이 새겨져 있다.

그 후 삼십여 년, 자기 주변의 모든 것은 변하여 갔지만 시계만은 옛 모습 그대로다. 주변뿐만 아니라 자기 자신은 얼마나 변한 것인가. 이십 대 홍안을 자랑하던 젊음은 어디로 사라진 것인지 머리카락도 반백이 넘었고 이마의 주름은 깊어만 간다. 일제시대, 소련군 점령하의 감옥 생활, 6·25 사변, 38선, 미군 부대, 그동안 몇 차례의 아슬아슬한 죽음의 고비를 넘긴 것인가.

Yi Inguk, M.D., drew an eighteen-carat-gold pocket watch from his vest and checked the time.

Two-forty.

Only twenty minutes until his appointment with Mr. Brown at the American embassy. His watch had seen a lot of history and could tell many tales. Whenever Yi Inguk, M.D., consulted it, he recalled one or another of the near-miraculous turns his life had taken. He had taken the watch when he crossed the thirty-eighth parallel as a refugee with only his black bag in hand. And now that he had replaced the old bag with a new one given to him by an American army doctor, the watch was the only remaining object that had escaped with him. It was, in a sense, his life's companion.

When he went to bed at night, he never placed it by his bedside or even left it in his vest pocket. He would always be sure to take it out and tuck it away inside the steel safe where he kept his registration papers, bank book, and other valuables. Indeed, he had good reason to do so. The watch was a prize of honor he had received on graduation from the Imperial University. His name was engraved on the back.

No matter what changes had swirled about him

'월삼 십칠석.[2]

　우여곡절 많은 세월 속에서 아직도 제 시간을 유지하는 것만도 신기하다. 시간을 보고는 습성처럼 째각째각 소리에 귀 기울이는 때의 그의 가느다란 눈매에는 흘러간 인생의 축도가 서리는 것이었고, 그 속에서는 각모(角帽)[3]와 쓰메에리[4] 학생복을 벗어 버리고 신사복으로 갈아입던 그날의 감회를 더욱 새롭게 해주는 충동을 금할 길 없는 것이었다.

　이인국 박사는 수술 직전에 서랍에 집어 넣었던 편지에 생각이 미쳤다.

　미국에 가 있는 딸 나미. 본래의 이름은 일본식의 나미꼬(奈美子)다. 해방 후 그것이 거슬린다기에 나미로 불렸고 새로 기류계[5]에 올릴 때에는 꼬[子] 자를 완전히 떼어버렸다.

　나미쌍! 딸의 모습은 단란하던 지난날의 추억과 더불어 떠올랐다.

　온 집안의 재롱둥이였던 나미, 그도 이젠 성숙했다. 그마저 자기 옆에서 떠난 지금 새로운 정에서 산다고는 하지만 이인국 박사는 가끔 물밀려오는 허전한 감을 금

18

these past thirty-odd years, his watch had always shown him a constant face. It wasn't only his surroundings—hadn't he himself changed, too? The proud and rosy-cheeked youth in his twenties had somehow disappeared, leaving this graying man with deepening wrinkles. The Japanese occupation, imprisonment under the Russians, the Korean War, the thirty-eighth parallel, the American army—how many crucial moments had he faced?

Waltham. Seventeen jewels.

It was nothing short of marvelous that this watch could have managed to keep time through so many tortuous years. He would often look at the time only to find his ear drawn to the ticking of his watch, as if by habit. He would then begin to see, with narrowing eyes, a miniature of his bygone life. He couldn't escape the renewed vision he would find there of himself on the day he first put on the coat and tie of a gentleman in place of the familiar high-collared uniform and angular cap he had worn as a student.

Dr. Yi Inguk's thoughts turned to a letter he had tucked away in a drawer just before the operation.

His daughter, Nami, was in America. Her name

할 길 없었다.

아내는 거제도 수용소에 있을 때 죽었고 아들의 생사는 지금껏 알 길이 없다.

서울에서 다시 만나 후처로 들어온 혜숙(惠淑). 이십 년의 연령차에서 오는 세대의 거리감을 그는 억지로 부인해 본다. 그러나 혜숙의 피둥피둥한 탄력에 윤기가 더해 가는 살결에 비해 자기의 주름 잡힌 까칠한 피부는 육체적 위축감마저 느끼게 하는 때가 없지 않았다.

그들 사이에서 난 돌 지난 어린것, 앞날이 아득한 이 핏덩이만이 지금의 이인국 박사의 곁을 지켜주는 유일한 피붙이다.

이인국 박사는 기대와 호기에 찬 심정으로 항공우편의 피봉을 뜯었다.

전번 편지에서 가타부타 단안은 내리지 않고 잘 생각해서 결정하라고 한 그 후의 경과다.

'결국은 그렇게 되고야 마는 건가……'

그는 편지를 탁자 위에 밀어놓았다. 어쩌면 이러한 결말은 딸의 출국 이전에서부터 이미 싹튼 것인지도 모른다는 생각이 들었다.

대학에서 영문과를 택한 딸, 개인지도를 하여준 외인

had once been typically Japanese—Namiko. But he had dropped the *ko* for good when he filed his residence papers after Liberation, since such names had begun to sound awkward then.

Dear Nami, little Namiko! Thoughts of his daughter called back visions of the warm family circle of yesterday.

Nami, the charmer, the pet of the family, was now fully grown. Though it was natural for her to have left his side now and to live within a new affection, Yi Inguk, M.D., could not hold back the flood of loneliness that overcame him from time to time.

His wife had died in the wartime internment camp on Kŏje Island, and he still had no idea whether his son was living or dead.

Hyesuk, whom he had met again in Seoul, was his second wife. He strained to deny the difference the twenty years between them made, though it was a generation. But when he compared Hyesuk's resilient good health and firm, glowing skin with his own coarse and wrinkled flesh, there were times he felt the physical withering of age upon him. Their year-old baby, with its remote, unclear future, was the only blood kin remaining at the side of Yi Inguk, M.D.

교수, 스칼라십을 얻어준 것도 그고, 유학 절차의 재정 보증인을 알선해 준 것도 그가 아닌가, 우연한 일은 아니다.

그러나 시류에 따라 미국 유학을 해야만 한다고 주장한 것은 오히려 아버지 자기가 아닌가.

동양학을 연구하고 있는 외인 교수. 이왕이면 한국 여성과 결혼했으면 좋겠다던 솔직한 고백에, 자기의 학문을 위한 탁월한 견해라고 무심코 찬의를 표한 것도 자기가 아니던. 그것도 지금 생각하면 하나의 암시였음이 분명하지 않은가.

이인국 박사는 상아로 된 오존 파이프를 앞니에 힘을 주어 지그시 깨물며 눈을 감았다.

꼭 풀 쑤어 개 좋은 일을 한 것만 같은 분하고도 허황한 심정이다.

'코쟁이 사위.'

생각만 해도 전신의 피가 역류하는 것 같은 몸서리가 느껴졌다.

'더러운 년 같으니, 기어코……'

그는 큰기침을 내뱉었다.

그의 생각은 왜정시대 내선일체의 혼인론이 떠돌던

Yi Inguk, M.D., tore open the air mail envelope, his heart full of expectation and curiosity. This was the reply to his advice to think things over and not to leap to some sudden, irreversible decision.

Is that the way it's going to be, after all?

He slid the letter onto the table. The thought struck him that maybe this whole business had begun even before his daughter had left the country. It couldn't have been an accident. She chose to major in English at the school where the man had been a foreign visiting instructor. He must have found her the scholarship and then offered to be her sponsor. Of course. But hadn't he, her own father, encouraged this overseas study as being in keeping with the times?

And when the visiting instructor, a student of the East, had confessed he might like to marry a Korean girl, hadn't he actually given his unintended approval by suggesting it would be a boon to the instructor's studies? Shouldn't he have caught the hint? Yi Inguk, M.D., bit down firmly on the ivory mouthpiece of his ozone pipe and closed his eyes. He felt like a squanderer, angry and desolate.

A big-nose for a son-in-law!

His whole body shuddered with aversion at the

이야기에까지 꼬리를 물었다. 그때는 그것을 비방하거나 굴욕처럼 느끼지는 않았다. 오히려 당연한 것으로 해석했고 어찌 보면 우월한 것으로 생각하지 않았던가. 그런데 이 경우는…….

그는 딸의 편지 구절을 곱씹었다.

'애정에 국경이 있어요?'

이것은 벌써 진부하다. 아비도 학창 시절에 그런 풍조는 다 마스터했다. 건방지게, 이제 새삼스레 아비에게 설교조로…… 좀 더 솔직하지 못하고…….

그러니 외딸인 제가 그런 국제결혼의 시금석이 되겠단 말인가.

'아무튼 아버지께서 쉬 한번 오신다니 최종 결정은 아버지의 의향에 따라 결정할 예정입니다만…….'

그래 아버지가 안 가면 그대로 정하겠단 말인가.

이인국 박사는 일대잡종(一代雜種)의 유전법칙이 떠오르자 머리를 내저었다. '흰둥이 외손자', 생각만 해도 징그럽다.

그는 내던졌던 사진을 다시 집어 들었다.

대학 캠퍼스 같은 석조전의 거대한 건물, 그 앞의 정원, 뒤쪽에 짝을 지어 걸어가는 남녀 학생, 이 배경 속에

thought, as if his blood had suddenly run back-ward.

That little vixen.

He coughed heavily and spat.

His thoughts leaped back to all the fuss they had made over Japanese-Korean marriages during the occupation. Then such things weren't the makings of slander and humiliation. Rather, they were thought quite natural by many, if not possibly even a mark of distinction. But, then, in his daughter's case...

He read his daughter's letter over again.

"Can love know any national boundaries?"

A cheap, time-worn platitude. Daddy had mastered all those fashions, too, when he was a student. Impertinence. Taking this fresh, preaching tone with her own father. Couldn't she be more open about it? So she, an only daughter, expects to experiment in international marriage?

"Anyway, since you said you could easily come overseas sometime, Father, I certainly want to hear your views before making any final decisions. However..."

So if Daddy doesn't go, she'll do as she pleases!

Yi Inguk, M.D., shook his head as he called to mind the laws of heredity for a first hybrid genera-

딸과 그 외인 교수가 나란히 어깨를 짚고 서서 웃음을 짓고 있다.

'흥, 놀기는 잘들 논다…….'

웅, 신음 소리를 치며 그는 자리에서 일어섰다. 아무튼 미스터 브라운을 만나 이왕 가는 길이면 좀 더 서둘러야겠다. 그 가장 대우가 좋다는 국무성 초청 케이스의 확정 여부를 빨리 확인해야겠다는 생각이 조바심을 쳤다.

그는 아내 혜숙이 있는 살림방 쪽으로 건너갔다.

"여보, 나미가 기어코 결혼하겠다는구려."

"그래요?"

아내의 어조에는 별다른 감동이나 의아도 없음을 이인국 박사는 직감했다.

그는 가능한 한 혜숙이 앞에서 전실 소생의 애들 이야기를 하는 것을 삼가왔다.

어떻게 보면 나미의 미국 유학을 간접적으로 자극한 것은 가정 분위기의 소치라는 자격지심이 없지 않기도 했다.

나미는 물론 혜숙을 단 한 번도 어머니라고 불러준 일이 없었다.

tion. A white grandson—the very thought disgusted him.

He picked up the discarded letter once again.

A large stone building on a landscaped campus and, in the background of the picture, boys and girls strolling in pairs; in the midst of this, his daughter and that foreign instructor standing side by side, smiling, with their arms around each other's shoulders.

Hmm. They certainly seem to be enjoying themselves.

He moaned and got up from the sofa. He had to hurry to avoid being late to Mr. Brown's. His anxieties were heightened as he thought how important the State Department invitation had become for him now.

He went back into the living quarters where his wife, Hyesuk, was waiting.

"Dear, it seems Nami has her heart set on getting married."

"Oh, really?"

Yi Inguk, M.D., quickly sensed the lack of any real concern in her voice. He was as careful as possible of what he said in front of Hyesuk about the children of his first wife. He really had to reproach himself for the atmosphere at home, which had

혜숙 또한 나미 앞에서 어머니라고 버젓이 행세한 일도 없었다.

지난날의 간호원과 오늘의 어머니, 그 사이에는 따져서 표현할 수 없는 미묘한 감정들이 복재[6]되어 있었다.

"선생님의 일이라면 무엇이든지 돕겠어요."

서울에서 이인국 박사를 다시 만났을 때 마음속 그대로 털어놓는 혜숙의 첫마디였다.

처음에는 혜숙도 부인의 별세를 몰랐고 이인국 박사도 혜숙의 혼인 여부를 참견하지 않았다.

혜숙은 곧 대학병원을 그만두고 이리로 옮겨왔다.

나미는 옛 정이 다시 살아 혜숙을 언니처럼 따랐다.

이들의 혼인이 익어갈 때 이인국 박사는 목에 걸리는 딸의 의향을 우선 듣기로 했다.

딸도 아버지의 외로움을 동정하고 있었다. 자기 자신 아버지의 시중이 힘에 겨웠고 또 그 사이 실지의 아버지 뒤치다꺼리를 혜숙이 해왔으므로 딸은 즉석에서 진심으로 찬의를 표했다.

그러나 시간이 흐를수록 혜숙과 나미의 간격은 벌어졌고 혜숙도 남편과의 정상적인 가정생활에 나미가 장애물이 되는 것 같은 느낌을 차츰 가지게 되었다.

been part of the reason for Nami's decision to study in the United States. Nami, of course, had never once called Hyesuk *Mother*. And Hyesuk, for her part, had quite fairly avoided asserting herself as a mother in front of Nami. Inexpressibly subtle and delicate feelings lay hidden in the relationship between Nami and today's mother, who was yesterday's nurse.

"I'm ready to help you in any way I can."

It was with these words that Hyesuk had opened up her heart to Yi Inguk, M.D., when they had met again in Seoul. At first, Hyesuk did not know of his first wife's death; nor did Yi Inguk, M.D., pry into Hyesuk's marital status. Hyesuk soon quit her job at the university hospital and came over to the clinic.

For Nami, it was a revival of old affections, and she clung to Hyesuk as to an older sister. When Yi Inguk, M.D., found himself on the brink of a new marriage, thoughts of his daughter's reaction made him seek out her opinion first.

She had sympathy for the loneliness he felt. And she was quick to sincerely praise his choice of a wife, since she knew that he needed more attention than she alone could give and also that Hyesuk had actually been doing much to raise his spirits. But as

혜숙 자신도 처음에는 마음 놓고 이인국 박사를 남편
이랍시고 일대일로 부르진 못했다.

나미의 출발, 그 후 어린애의 해산, 이러한 몇 고개를
넘는 사이에 이제 겨우 아내답게 늠름히 남편을 대할
수 있고 이인국 박사 또한 제대로의 남편의 체모[7]로 아
내에게 농을 걸 수도 있게끔 되었다.

"기어쿠 그 외인 교수하군가 가까워지는 모양인데."

이인국 박사는 아내의 얼굴을 직시하지는 못하고 마
치 독백하듯이 뇌까렸다.

"할 수 있어요, 제 좋다는 대로 해야지요."

마치 남의 이야기를 하는 것처럼 이인국 박사에게는
들려왔다.

"글쎄, 하기는 그렇지만……."

그는 입맛만 다시며 더 이상 계속하지 못했다.

잠을 깨어 울고 있는 어린것에게 젖을 물리고 있는
아내의 젊은 육체에서 자극을 느끼면서 이인국 박사는
자기 자신이 죄를 지은 것만 같은 나미에 대한 강박관
념을 금할 길이 없었다.

저 어린것이 자라서 아들 원식(元植)이나 또 나미 정
도의 말상대가 되려도 아직 이십여 년의 세월이 흘러야

time passed, Hyesuk and Nami became more distant, and Hyesuk began to feel that Nami stood in the way of a normal family life for herself and her husband.

Hyesuk had found it impossible at first to feel at ease with Yi Inguk, M.D., in her new role as his wife. But with Nami's departure, the birth of the child, and other things, she reached the point where she could just manage to be a wife to him. Yi Inguk, M.D., for his part, even learned to become a familiar, joking husband.

"She really seems to be getting serious about that foreign instructor."

Yi Inguk, M.D., avoided direct contact with his wife's eyes and repeated his words as if grumbling to himself.

"That can happen. I suppose she should do as she likes."

To Yi Inguk, M.D., her voice sounded as though she were talking about a stranger.

"Well, she's doing that all right, but..."

He tutted, unable to continue.

He was aroused by the sight of his wife's young body as she gave her breast to the crying baby, who had just woken up. But at the same time he

한다.

　그때 자기는 칠십이 넘는 할아버지다.

　현대 의학이 인간의 평균 수명을 연장하고, 암(癌) 같은 고질이 아닌 한 불의의 죽음은 없다 하지만, 자기 자신이 의사이면서 스스로의 생명 하나를 보장할 수 없다.

　'마누라는 눈앞에서 나는 새 놓치듯이 죽이지 않았던가.'

　아무리 해도 저놈이 대학을 나올 때까지는 살아야 한다. 아무렴, 때가 때인 만큼 미국 유학까지는 내 생전에 시켜주어야 하지.

　하기야 그런 의미에서도 일찌감치 미국 혼반[8]을 맺어두는 것도 그리 해로울 건 없지 않나. 아무렴, 우리보다는 낫게 사는 사람들인데. 좀 남보기 체면이 안 서서 그렇지.

　그는 자위인지 체념인지 모를 푸념을 곱씹었다.

　"여보, 저걸 좀 꾸려요."

　이인국 박사의 말씨는 점잖게 가라앉았다.

　"뭐 말이에요?"

　아내는 젖꼭지를 물린 채 고개만을 돌려 되묻는다.

felt overwhelmed by an obsessive sense of guilt toward his daughter, Nami.

He still had some twenty years to wait before this child would be old enough to talk with as he could talk with Nami or his son, Wŏnshik. Come that day, he'd be an old man in his seventies. Modern medicine had extended man's life span and, except for things like cancer, even eliminated sudden death; still, a doctor couldn't guarantee his own life.

Didn't I let my wife die in front of my eyes as easily as I would let a bird take flight?

At any rate, he had to live until that child made it through college. Indeed, if he lasted long enough he'd have to see the boy through to study in the United States.

When he thought of things in that light, getting started early as a member of an American family did not seem such a bad idea. No question that they live better than Koreans do. It's just that it's difficult to keep from losing face with others.

So he mulled his problems over—whether he was consoling himself or simply resigned, he didn't really know.

"Dear, would you wrap that up for me?"

Dr. Yi Inguk's voice had taken a gentle turn.

"저, 병 말이오."

그는 화장대 위에 놓은 골동품을 가리켰다.

"어디 가져가셔요?"

"저 미 대사관 브라운 씨 말이야. 늘 신세만 졌는데……."

아내가 꼼꼼히 싸놓은 포장물을 들고 이인국 박사는 천천히 현관을 나섰다.

벌써 석간신문이 배달되었다.

아무리 생각해도 그것은 분명 기적임에 틀림없는 일이었다. 간헐적으로 반복되어 공포와 감격을 함께 휘몰아치는 착잡한 추억. 늘 어제 일마냥 생생하기만 하다.

1945년 팔월 하순.

아직 해방의 감격이 온 누리를 뒤덮어 소용돌이칠 때였다.

말복도 지난 날씨건만 여전히 무더웠다. 이인국 박사는 이 며칠 동안 불안과 초조에 휘몰려 잠도 제대로 자지 못했다. 무엇인가 닥쳐올 사태를 오돌오돌 떨면서 대기하는 상태였다.

그렇게 붐비던 환자도 하나 얼씬하지 않고 쉴 사이

"Wrap what up?"

His wife turned her head toward him, letting the child nurse undisturbed at her breast.

"That vase, there."

He pointed to an antique standing on his wife's dressing table.

"Where are you taking it?"

"To that Mr. Brown at the American embassy. I'm so indebted to him now."

Yi Inguk, M.D., carrying the package neatly wrapped by his wife, stepped out into the front hall. The evening paper had already been delivered.

No matter how you look at it, his survival had to be a miracle. The confused recollection could still whip up alternating feelings of fear and gratitude— so vivid that the event always seemed like yesterday to him.

Late August 1945. Strong emotions were sweeping over the world and churning up whirlpools as they spread. The dog days were nearly over, but the weather was as hot and sultry as ever. For some days, Yi Inguk, M.D., driven by feelings of anxiety and impatience, had found normal sleep impossible. He could only quiver with tension as he

없던 전화도 뜸하여졌다. 입원실은 최후의 복막염 환자였던 도청의 일본인 과장이 끌려간 후 텅 비었다.

조수와 약제사는 궁금증이 나서 고향에 다녀오겠다고 떠나갔고, 서울 태생인 간호원 혜숙만이 남아 빈집 같은 병원을 지키고 있었다.

이층 십 조 다다미방에 훈도시[9]와 유카다[10] 바람에 뒹굴고 있던 이인국 박사는 견디다 못해 부채를 내던지고 일어났다.

그는 목욕탕으로 갔다. 찬물을 퍼서 대야째로 머리에서부터 몇 번이고 내리부었다. 등줄기가 시리고 몸이 가벼워졌다.

그러나 수건으로 몸을 닦으면서도 무엇엔가 짓눌려 있는 것 같은 가슴속의 갑갑증을 가서 낼 수가 없었다.

그는 창문으로 기웃이 한길 가를 내려다보았다. 우글거리는 군중들은 아직도 소음 속으로 밀려가고 있다.

굳게 닫혀 있는 은행 철문에 붙은 벽보가 한길을 건너 하얀 윤곽만이 두드러져 보인다.

아니 그곳에 씌어 있는 구절.

親日派, 民族反逆者를 打倒하자.

waited for the coming of whatever was approaching.

No sign was left of the many patients who used to come and go, and the once restless telephone now waited silently. All the rooms were empty and echoing, now that the last patient—a Japanese section chief from the provincial administration who had been ill with peritonitis—had been taken away.

The assistants and pharmacists had all given in to anxiety and left, saying they would return after visiting their hometowns. Only the Seoul-born nurse Hyesuk remained to watch over the empty clinic.

In the ten-mat tatami room upstairs, Yi Inguk, M.D., clad in Japanese breechcloth and kimono, could toss and turn no more. He finally threw aside his fan and got up.

He went into the bathroom. He scooped up cold water by the basinful and poured it over his head, letting it flow down the length of his body. A chill traveled down his backbone, and he felt lighter. But while he could wipe his body with the washcloth, he could not wash away the uncertain and oppressive disquiet in his heart.

He glanced out the window at the streets below. Swarms of people were still surging back and forth,

옆에 붉은 동그라미를 두 겹으로 친 글자가 그대로 눈앞에 선명하게 보이는 것만 같다.

어제 저물녘에 그것을 처음 보았을 때의 전율이 되살아왔다.

순간 이인국 박사는 방 쪽으로 머리를 획 돌렸다.

'나야 원 괜찮겠지……'

혼자 뇌까리면서 그는 다시 부채를 들었다. 그러나 벽보를 들여다보고 있을 때 자기와 눈이 마주치는 순간, 일그러지는 얼굴에 경멸인지 통쾌인지 모를 웃음을 비죽거리면서 아래위로 훑어보던 그 춘석(春錫)이 녀석의 모습이 자꾸만 머릿속으로 엄습하여 어두운 밤에 거미줄을 뒤집어쓴 것처럼 꺼림텁텁하기만 했다.

그깟 놈 하고 머리에서 씻어버리려도 거머리처럼 자꾸만 감아 붙는 것만 같았다.

벌써 육 개월 전의 일이다.

형무소에서 병보석으로 가출옥되었다는 중환자가 업혀서 왔다.

휑뎅그런 눈에 앙상하게 뼈만 남은 몸을 제대로 가누

engulfed in their own noise. From across the street, a poster pasted on the tightly closed iron doors of a bank appeared only as a square of white to him. But what they'd written there...

"Destroy Pro-Japanese and Betrayers of the People!"

All he could see clearly from where he stood were the red circles that marked either end of the slogan. He felt once more the shiver that had gone through him the previous night when he saw it for the first time. Yi Inguk, M.D., instantly turned his head toward the room again.

Why, they certainly wouldn't touch me.

He repeated this to himself as he picked up the fan again. But he had been made extremely uneasy by something that had happened while he was down there, looking at the poster. As he withdrew his intent gaze from the slogan, his eyes met those of that troublemaker Ch'unsŏk, who looked him up and down, sneering with that distorted look that could have meant contempt or delight, for all he knew. The unnerving image of that encounter had taken to attacking his memory without warning, like a spider web that entangles you in the dark of night.

As much as he tried to wipe that Ch'unsŏk out of his thoughts, the fellow would always be there,

지도 못하는 환자, 그는 간호원의 부축으로 겨우 진찰을 받았다.

청진기의 상아 꼭지를 환자의 가슴에서 등으로 옮겨 두 줄기의 고무줄에서 감득되는 숨소리를 감별하면서도, 이인국 박사의 머릿속은 최후 판정의 분기점을 방황하고 있었다.

'입원시킬 것인가, 거절할 것인가…….'

환자의 몰골이나 업고 온 사람의 옷매무새로 보아 경제 정도는 뻔한 일이라 생각되었다.

그러나 그것보다도 더 마음에 켕기는 것이 있었다. 일본인 간부급들이 자기 집처럼 들락날락하는 이 병원에 이런 사상범을 입원시킨다는 것은 관선 시의원이라는 체면에서도 떳떳지 못할뿐더러, 자타가 공인하는 모범적인 황국신민(皇國臣民)의 공든 탑이 하루아침에 무너지는 결과를 가져오는 것이라는 생각이 들었다.

순간 그는 이런 경우의 가부 결정에 일도양단하는 자기 식으로 찰나적인 단안을 내렸다.

그는 응급치료만 하여주고 입원실이 없다는 가장 떳떳하고도 정당한 구실로 애걸하는 환자를 돌려보냈다.

환자의 집이 병원에서 멀지 않은 건너편 골목 안에

clinging like a leech.

It had happened six months before.

A critically ill patient was carried in from a prison, freed temporarily for treatment, they explained. The helpless youth was but a gaunt, emaciated frame punctuated by a pair of vacant eyes. He could hardly shift his body for the examination without help from the nurse.

As he moved the ivory tip of his stethoscope from the patient's chest to his back and tried to make out the sound of breathing through the rubber tubes, Dr. Yi Inguk's mind wandered to thoughts of the Last Judgment.

Should he be taken in? Should he be turned away?

A glance at the patient's appearance and at the clothing of the man who had carried him in easily revealed his economic status.

But this time something else disturbed him. Not only did it seem improper for him, as a government-appointed City Assemblyman, to admit this political criminal to a clinic patronized by leading Japanese officials; but he also feared that the monument of his good works, for which he was officially recognized as a model citizen of the Empire,

있다는 것은 후에 간호원에게서 들었다. 그러나 그쯤은 예사로운 일이었기에 그는 그대로 아무렇지도 않게 흘려버렸다.

그런데 며칠 전 시민대회 끝에 있은 해방 경축 시가행진을 자기도 흥분에 차 구경하느라고 혜숙과 함께 대문 앞에 나갔다가, 자위대 완장(腕章)을 두르고 대열에 낀 젊은이와 눈이 마주쳤다.

이쪽을 노려보는 청년의 눈에서 불똥이 튀는 것 같은 살기를 느꼈다.

무슨 영문인지 모르고 어리벙벙하던 이인국 박사는 그것이 언젠가 입원을 거절당한 사상범 환자 춘석이라는 것을 혜숙에게서 듣고야 슬금슬금 주위의 눈치를 살피며 집으로 기어 들어왔다.

그 후 그는 될 수 있는 대로 거리로 나가는 것을 피하였지마는 공교롭게도 어젯저녁에 그 벽보 앞에서 마주쳤었다.

갑자기 밖이 와자지껄 떠들어대었다. 머리에 깍지를 끼고 비스듬히 누워서 갈피를 잡을 수 없는 생각에 골똘하던 이인국 박사는 일어나 앉아 한길 쪽에 귀를 기

could come crashing down overnight because of something like this.

As was his style, he weighed the facts and, in an instant, rendered an immediate and incisive decision. He gave only emergency treatment and sent the supplicant on his way with the very reasonable and proper excuse that there was no room for him at the clinic. He learned later from the nurse that the patient's house was in an alley across the street from the clinic. But since such things were common for him, he dismissed it as a trifle.

Then, just a few days earlier, caught up in the enthusiasm of the moment, he and Hyesuk had stepped out front of the clinic to watch the parade following a mass rally to celebrate Liberation. His eyes happened to meet those of a young marcher wearing the armband of the Self-defense Corps. He felt as if the young man were shooting sparks with those relentless eyes.

The bewildered Yi Inguk, M.D., had no idea of the reason for this until Hyesuk told him that the marcher was Ch'unsŏk, the political offender who had once been turned away from the clinic. Hearing this, he looked furtively from face to face around him and slipped back into the clinic. After that, he

울렸다. 들끓는 소리는 더 커갔다. 궁금증에 견디다 못해 그는 엉거주춤 꾸부린 자세로 밖을 내다보았다. 포도에 뒤끓는 사람들은 손에 손에 태극기와 적기(赤旗)를 들고 환성을 울리고 있었다.

'무엇일까?'

그는 고개를 갸웃하며 다시 자리에 주저앉았다.

계단을 구르며 급히 올라오는 발자국 소리가 들려왔다.

혜숙이다.

"아마 소련군이 들어오나 봐요. 모두들 야단법석이에요……."

숨을 헐레벌떡이며 이야기하는 혜숙의 말에 이인국 박사는 아무 대꾸도 없이 눈만 껌벅이며 도로 앉았다. 여러 날째 라디오에서 오늘 입성 예정이라고 했으니 인제 정말 오는가 보다 싶었다.

혜숙이 내려간 뒤에도 이인국 박사는 한참 동안 아무 거동도 못 하고 바깥쪽을 내려다보고만 있었다.

무엇을 생각했던지 그는 움찔 자리에서 일어났다. 그러고는 벽장문을 열었다. 안쪽에 손을 뻗쳐 액자틀을 끄집어내었다.

had avoided going out into the streets as much as possible, only to run into Ch'unsŏk again in front of the poster the previous night.

Suddenly a clamor arose outside. Yi Inguk, M.D., who had been lost in aimless reveries as he lay with his hands clasped behind his head, sat up and turned an ear toward the street. The commotion grew even louder. Unable to suppress his anxiety any longer, he rose and, squatting by the window, looked down into the street. Outside, the seething crowds were waving Korean and Russian flags as they raised great shouts of joy.

What could this be?

He cocked his head in wonder as he sank down to a sitting position. Hearing the sound of footsteps, he rose as someone came hurrying up the stairs. It was Hyesuk.

"I think maybe the Russian army's coming into town! Everybody's out there carrying on."

Yi Inguk, M.D., gave no response to Hyesuk's breathless report. He only blinked and sat back down. For some time now the radio had been predicting that the Russians would enter the city today. So it seems they're really here. For some time after

國語常用의 家.

해방되던 날 떼어서 집어넣어둔 것을 그동안 깜박 잊고 있었다.

그는 액자틀 뒤를 열어 음식점 면허장 같은 두터운 모조지를 빼내어 글자 한 자도 제대로 남지 않게 손끝에 힘을 주어 꼼꼼히 찢었다.

이 종잇장 하나만 해도 일본인과의 교제에 있어서 얼마나 떳떳한 구실을 할 수 있었던 것인가. 야릇한 미련 같은 것이 섬광처럼 머릿속에 스쳐갔다.

환자도 일본말 모르는 축은 거의 오는 일이 없었지만 대외관계는 물론 집 안에서도 일체 일본말만을 써왔다. 해방 뒤 부득이 써오는 제 나라 말이 오히려 의사표현에 어색함을 느낄 만큼 그에게는 거리가 먼 것이었다.

마누라의 솔선수범하는 내조지공도 컸지만 애들까지도 곧잘 지켜주었기에 이 종잇장을 탄 것이 아니던가. 그것을 탄 날은 온 집안이 무슨 큰 경사나 난 것처럼 기뻐들 했었다.

"잠꼬대까지 국어로 할 정도가 아니면 이 영예로운 기회야 얻을 수 있겠소."

Hyesuk had gone back down, Yi Inguk, M.D., sat there looking numbly out the window.

Stirred into action by a passing thought, he suddenly got up. He then slid open the door of a small closet. He reached deep into its recesses and drew out a framed Japanese document.

National Language Family.

He had completely forgotten about this award since taking it down and putting it away in the closet on the day of Liberation from Japan.

He opened the frame from the back and, removing the heavy vellum sheet, which looked like a restaurant license, carefully tore the document into such fine shreds that not one letter was left legible. This one sheet of paper could demonstrate how honorable his relationship with the Japanese was. An odd melancholy flashed through his mind.

Few of his patients had ever come from the groups that couldn't speak Japanese. Not only had he always spoken the national language in the clinic and throughout his social life, but he had also insisted on using Japanese exclusively at home, too. So unfamiliar had he become with Korean that he had found it awkward to express himself in it after Liberation.

하던 국민총력연맹 지부장의 웃음 띤 치하 소리가 떠올랐다.

그 순간, 자기 자신은 아이들을 소학교부터 일본 학교에 보낸 것을 얼마나 다행으로 여겼던 것인가.

그는 후 한숨을 내뿜었다. 그리고 저금통장의 잔액을 깡그리 내주던 은행 지점장의 호의에 새삼 고마움을 느끼는 것이었다.

그것마저 없었더라면…… 등골에 오싹하는 한기가 느껴왔다.

무슨 정치가 오든 그것만 있으면 시내 사람의 절반 이상이 굶어 죽기 전에야 우리 집 차례는 아니겠지. 그는 손금고가 들어 있는 안방 단스[11]를 생각하면서 혼자 중얼거렸다.

이인국 박사는 무슨 일이 일어나도 꼭 자기만은 살아남을 것 같은 막연한 기대를 곱씹고 있다.

주위가 어두워 왔다.

지축이 흔들리는 것 같은 동요와 소음이 가까워졌다. 군중들의 환호성이 터져 나왔다. 만세 소리가 연방 계속되었다.

세상 형편을 알아보려고 거리에 나갔던 아내가 돌아

His wife had contributed a great deal toward winning this award by her efforts to set an example for others. Even the children had done their part in maintaining the spirit. On the day of the award, the entire household celebrated the occasion as joyfully as it might a birth or another happy family event.

"You use the national language so faithfully that you must surely speak it in your sleep! How else could this honor have come to you?"

The sound of those complimentary remarks, made that day by the smiling officer from the local branch of the Citizens League for Total Effort, came floating back to him. Hadn't he at that moment even reflected on how fortunate it had been for him to have given his children a Japanese education from elementary school on?

He heaved a long sigh. He had just recalled with gratitude the helpful branch manager of the bank who had let him withdraw the entire balance in his savings account. What if he didn't have that with him now? He felt a chill creep down his spine. Whatever became of the government, as long as he had the cash in hand half the people in the city could starve to death before his family was touched. He mumbled to himself as he thought of the cashbox

왔다.

"여보, 땅꾸 부대가 들어왔어요. 거리는 온통 사람들 사태가 났는데 집 안에 처박혀 뭘 하구 있어요."

"뭘 하기는?"

"나가 보아요, 마우재가 들어왔어요……."

어둠 속에서 아내의 음성은 격했으나 감격인지 당황인지 알 길이 없었다.

'계집이란 저렇게 우둔하구두 대담한 것일까……'

이인국 박사는 엷은 어둠 속에서 마누라 쪽을 주시하면서 입맛을 다셨다.

"불두 옆때 안 켜구."

마누라가 전등 스위치를 틀었다. 이인국 박사는 백 촉 전등의 너무 환한 것이 못마땅했다.

"불은 왜 켜는 거요?"

"그럼 켜지 않구, 캄캄한데…… 자, 어서 나가봅시다."

마누라의 이끄는 데 따라 이인국 박사는 마지못하면서 시침을 떼고 따라나섰다.

헤드라이트의 눈부신 광선. 탱크 부대의 진주는 끝을 알 수 없이 계속되고 있다.

이인국 박사는 부신 불빛을 피하면서 가로수에 기대

in the bedroom closet. Yi Inguk, M.D., mulled over his vague concern that, somehow, he had to survive, come what may.

The day around him grew darker.

As a distant rumble approached, the earth itself seemed to shudder on its axis. The crowds outside exploded into round after round of cheers. His wife came back in from the street.

"Dear, there's a tank unit in town, and the streets are just packed with people! Whatever are you doing here all alone in the house?"

"What am I doing?"

"Come out and see, dear! The *Russkis* are here!"

In the darkness he couldn't tell why his wife's voice seemed to tremble, whether from emotion or bewilderment. *Can women really be so silly and yet so fearless at the same time?* Yi Inguk, M.D., peered in his wife's direction across the dim room and clucked.

"Why, you haven't even turned the light on yet!"

His wife snapped the switch on the lamp. The brightness of the 100-watt bulb was too much for Yi Inguk, M.D.

"What are you turning the light on for?"

"All right, leave it off and sit in the dark, then.

어 섰다. 박수와 환호성, 만세 소리가 그칠 줄 모르는 양안(兩岸)을 끼고 탱크는 물밀듯 서서히 흘러간다. 위 뚜껑을 열고 반신을 내민 중대가리의 병정은 간간이, '우라아' 하면서 손을 내흔들고 있다.

이인국 박사는 자기와는 아무 관련도 없는 이방 부대라는 환각을 느끼면서 박수도 환성도 안 나가는 멋쩍은 속에서 멍하니 쳐다보고만 있다. 그는 자기의 거동을 주시하지나 않나 해서 주위를 두리번거렸다.

그러나 아무도 그에게는 관심을 두는 일 없이 탱크를 향하여 목청이 터지도록 거듭 만세만 부르고 있지 않은가.

'어떻게 되겠지…….'

그는 밑도 끝도 없는 한마디를 뇌면서 유유히 집으로 들어왔다.

민요 뒤에 계속되던 행진곡이 그치고 주둔군 사령관의 포고문이 방송되고 있다.

이인국 박사는 라디오 앞에 다가앉아 귀를 기울였다.

시민의 생명 재산은 절대 보장한다, 각자는 안심하고 자기의 직장을 수호하라, 총기(銃器), 일본도(日本刀) 등 일체의 무기 소지는 금하니 즉시 반납하라는 등의 요지

Come on now, come along outside!"

Yi Inguk, M.D., had no choice but to follow his insistent wife, feigning indifference as he went.

Blazing headlights dazzled the eyes of the onlookers as the endless column of tanks rumbled by. Yi Inguk, M.D., leaned against a wayside tree, avoiding the glare. The tanks rolled on slowly like a rising tide between two heaving banks of cheering, clapping, shouting people. The Russian soldiers, standing waist deep in the hatchways of their tanks, waved and called "*Urra*" from time to time.

Yi Inguk, M.D., stood staring blankly and awkwardly, unable to clap or cheer as he nursed the illusion that these foreign soldiers had nothing to do with him or his life. He glanced at the crowd around him, wondering if perhaps his behavior had attracted attention. But no one seemed to be taking any interest in him; all eyes were on the passing tanks as the onlookers cheered themselves hoarse.

What's to come of this?

He repeated this question, to which there was neither end nor answer, as he went slowly back into the house.

On the radio, the folksongs and marches were over now and the commander of the Army of Oc-

였다.

그는 문득 단스 속에 넣어둔 엽총(獵銃)에 생각이 미치었다. 그러면 저것도 바쳐야 하는 것일까. 영국제 쌍발, 손때 묻은 애완물같이 느껴져 누구에게 단 한 번 빌려주지 않았던 최신형 특제품이다.

이인국 박사는 다이얼을 돌렸다. 대체 서울에서는 어떻게들 하고 있는 것일까.

거기도 마찬가지다. 민요가 아니면 행진곡이 나오고 그러다가는 건국준비위원회 누구인가의 연설이 계속된다.

대체 앞으로 어떻게 될 것인가 궁금증을 해결할 방법이 없다.

해방 직후 이삼 일 동안은 자기도 태연하였지만 번지르르하게 드나들던 몇몇 친구들도 소련군 입성이 보도된 이후부터는 거의 나타나질 않는다. 그렇다고 자기 자신이 뛰어다니며 물을 경황은 더욱 없다.

밤이 이슥해서야 중학교와 국민학교를 다니는 아들딸이 굉장한 구경이나 한 것처럼 탱크와 로스케[12]의 이야기를 늘어놓으며 돌아왔다.

그들은 아버지의 심중은 아랑곳없다는 듯이 어머니,

cupation was making a proclamation. Yi Inguk, M.D., sat down in front of the radio and brought his ear up close to the speaker.

The army guaranteed the lives and property of the populace, announced a strict prohibition on the possession of swords and firearms (which had to be turned in), and requested all citizens to remain calm and conduct business as usual.

He suddenly thought of the hunting rifle he kept in the bedroom closet. Would he have to turn it in? It was the newest model, a double-barreled British shotgun that bore the sweat of his own hands. Did he really have to give up this beloved treasure, which he had never once even loaned out?

Yi Inguk, M.D., turned the radio dial. What could they be doing in Seoul now? Same story there, too. If not folksongs, then marches, followed by speeches by someone or other from the Preparatory Committee for National Foundation.

How on earth was this all going to end? There seemed to be no relief from the anxiety this question stirred up in him. He had been calm and composed for two or three days after Liberation, but then, after the announcement of the arrival of the Russians, even those friends who used to pop in

혜숙과 함께 저희들 이야기에만 꽃을 피우고 있었다.

이인국 박사는 슬그머니 일어나 이층으로 올라와 다다미방에서 혼자 뒹굴었다.

앞일은 대체 어떻게 전개될 것인지, 뛰어넘을 수가 없는 큰 바다가 가로놓인 것만 같았다. 풀어낼 수 있는 실마리가 전연 더듬어지지 않는 뒤헝클어진 상념 속에서 그대로 이인국 박사는 꺼지려는 짚불을 불어 일으키는 심정으로 막연한 한 가닥의 기대만을 끝내 포기하지 않은 채 천장을 멍청히 쳐다보고만 있었다.

지난 일에 대한 뉘우침이나 가책 같은 건 아예 있을 수 없었다.

자동차 속에서 이인국 박사는 들고 나온 석간을 펼쳤다.

일면의 제목을 대강 훑고 난 그는 신문을 뒤집어 꺾어 삼면으로 눈을 옮겼다.

北韓 蘇聯留學生 西獨으로 脫出.

바둑돌 같은 굵은 활자의 제목. 왼편 전단을 차지한

and out all the time stopped appearing. And he was growing less and less interested in the idea of running around to ask after them.

It wasn't until late at night that his middle school son and primary school daughter had come home, bursting with talk of the *Russkis* and their tanks, as if they had seen something quite colossal. Their father didn't seem at all interested in listening, but their stories flourished and multiplied as they shared them with their mother and Hyesuk.

Yi Inguk, M.D., had gotten up and slipped out of the room. He went upstairs to the tatami-matted second floor, where he tossed and turned alone. How were things going to work out? The future seemed to spread out before him like a vast ocean that he could never cross. His thoughts were a tangle of string that wouldn't yield up a free end—he could only stare dumbly at the ceiling, nursing vague hopes as if blowing on a dying ember. Guilt or regret for bygone acts was simply beside the point.

Inside the car, Yi Inguk, M.D., opened up the evening paper he had taken from the house. After glancing over the headlines, he folded the paper

외신 기사. 손바닥만 한 사진까지 곁들여 있다.

그는 코허리에 내려온 안경을 올리면서 눈을 부릅떴다.

그의 시각은 활자 속을 헤치고, 머릿속에는 아들의 환상이 뒤엉켜 들어차 왔다. 아들을 모스크바로 유학시킨 것은 자기의 억지에서였던 것만 같았다.

출신계급, 성분, 어디 하나나 부합될 조건이 있었단 말인가. 고급 중학을 졸업하고 의과대학에 입학된 바로 그해다.

이인국 박사는 그때나 지금이나 자기의 처세 방법에 대하여 절대적인 자신을 가지고 있다.

"얘, 너 그 노어 공부를 열심히 해라."

"왜요?"

아들은 갑자기 튀어나오는 아버지의 말에 의아를 느끼면서 반문했다.

"야 원식아, 별수 없다. 왜정 때는 그래도 일본말이 출세를 하게 했고 이제는 노어가 또 판을 치지 않니. 고기가 물을 떠나서 살 수 없는 바에야 그 물 속에서 살 방도를 궁리해야지. 아무튼 그 노서아말 꾸준히 해라."

아들은 아버지 말에 새삼스러이 자극을 받는 것 같진

back to have a look at the miscellaneous items on page three.

North Korean Students in Russia Defect to West Germany.

Type as large as the pieces in a game of go topped a foreign dispatch that monopolized a full column at the left of the page. It was accompanied by a picture as big as the palm of your hand. He pushed his glasses back up on the bridge of his nose, from where they had slipped, and strained to read the text. His eyes dug through the fine print as a vision of his son rose to his mind's eye.

It seemed to him that his son's study in Moscow was the direct result of his own insistence. But was there any other way to overcome the limitations of his social origins and ideology? It was the year of his son's graduation from high school, the year he entered medical college. Yi Inguk, M.D., then as now, was quite confident that he knew how to run his son's life.

"You'd better work hard on your Russian, young man!"

"What for?"

The boy's only response to his father's sudden and suspicious comment was a question.

않았다.

"내 나이로도 인제 이만큼 뜨내기 회화쯤은 할 수 있는데, 새파란 너희 낫세[13]로야 그걸 못 하겠니."

"염려 마세요, 아버지……."

아들의 대답이 그에게는 믿음직스럽게 여겨졌다.

이인국 박사는 심각한 표정으로 말을 이었다.

"어디 코 큰 놈이라구 별것이겠니, 말 잘해서 진정이 통하기만 하면 그것들두 다 그렇지……."

이인국 박사는 끝내 스텐코프 소좌의 배경으로 요직에 있는 당 간부의 추천을 받아 아들의 소련 유학을 결정짓고야 말았다.

"여보, 보통으로 삽시다. 거저 표 나지 않게 사는 것이 이런 세상에선 가장 편안할 것 같아요. 이제 겨우 죽을 고비를 면했는데 또 쟤까지 그 '높이 드는' 복판에 휘몰아 넣으면 어쩔라구……."

"가만있어요. 호랑이두 굴에 가야 잡는 법이오. 무슨 세상이 되든 할 대로 해봅시다."

"그래도 저 어린것을 어떻게 노서아까지 보낸단 말이오."

"아니, 중학교 애들도 가지 못해 골들을 싸매는데, 대

"Now, Wŏnshik! There's no magic formula, you know. During the Japanese occupation you had to speak Japanese to get anywhere in spite of yourself. Today, it's Russian. Since a fish can't live out of water, he's got to think about surviving in the water, doesn't he? You've got to apply yourself to Russian."

The son didn't seem to be particularly inspired by his father's words.

"Here I've managed to pick up a smattering of conversation, even at my age. There's no reason why a youngster like you can't do it."

"Please, Father, don't worry about it anymore."

The answer sounded convincing enough to him. But Yi Inguk, M.D., continued to speak with an expression of grave concern on his face.

"Do you think there's anything special about them, except for their big noses? If you can just speak their language well enough to get your point across —they're the same as all the others."

Yi Inguk, M.D., had finally decided on a Russian education for his son when he happened to obtain a letter of recommendation from one of Major Stenkov's powerful connections in the Party leadership.

학생이 못 가 견딜라구."

"그래도 어디 앞일을 알겠소……."

"괜한 소리, 쟤가 소련 바람을 쏘이구 와야 내게 허튼
소리하는 놈들도 찍소리를 못 할 거요. 어디 보란 듯이
다시 한번 살아봅시다."

아들의 출발을 앞두고 걱정하는 마누라를 우격다짐
으로 무마시키고 그는 아들 유학을 관철하였다.

'흥, 혁명 유가족두 가기 힘든 구멍을 친일파 이인국
의 아들이 뚫었으니 어디 두구보자…….'

그는 만장의 기염을 토하며 혼자 중얼거리고는 희망
에 찬 미소를 풍겼다.

그 다음 해에 사변이 터졌다.

잘 있노라는 서신이 계속하여 왔지만 동란 후 후퇴할
때까지 소식은 두절된 대로였다.

마누라의 죽음은 외아들을 사지로 보낸 것 같은 수심
에도 그 원인이 있었다고 그는 생각하고 있다.

이인국 박사는 신문 다찌끼리[14] 속에 채워진 글자를
하나도 빼지 않고 다 훑어 내려갔다.

그러나 아들의 이름에 연관되는 사연은 한마디도 없
었다.

"Dear, let's live quietly, the way others do. In a world like this it's safest to keep a low profile. Here we have just barely managed to escape the threat of death, and now you want to push our boy into the middle of that 'Raise the Red Flag' business. If you succeed in this, what will become of him?"

"Listen, now. You can't catch a tiger without entering his lair. Whatever comes of the world, let's get what we can out of it."

"You mean to send the boy all the way to Russia?"

"Well, no. But lots of other middle school children are bearing down on their studies right now, even though they can't go abroad yet. Even college students don't find it all that easy."

"But still, how can you be so sure about the future?"

"Don't talk nonsense. Once that boy comes back with his Russian education, we won't hear a peep out of all those people who like to jabber so much about me. Let's live again as we did before, second to no one."

He browbeat his wife into agreement—in spite of her worries over such a venture—and then went on to complete the arrangements for his son's Russian education.

'이 자식은 무얼 꾸물꾸물하느라고 이런 축에도 끼지 못한담……. 사태를 판별하고 임기응변의 선수를 쓸 줄 알아야지, 맹추같이…….'

그는 신문을 포개어 되는대로 말아 쥐었다.

'개천에서 용마가 난다는데 이건 제 애비만도 못한 자식이야…….'

그는 혀를 찍찍 갈겼다.

'어쩌면 가족이 월남한 것조차 모르고 주저하고 있는 것이나 아닐까. 아니 이제는 그쪽에도 소식이 가서 제게도 무언중의 압력이 퍼져갈 터인데……. 역시 고지식한 놈이 아무래도 모자라…….'

그는 자동차에서 내리자 건 가래침을 내뱉었다.

'독또오루[15] 리, 내가 책임지고 보장하겠소. 아들을 우리 조국 소련에 유학시키시오.'

스텐코프의 목소리가 고막에 와 부딪는 것만 같았다.

자위대가 치안대로 바뀐 다음 날이다. 이인국 박사는 치안대에 연행되었다.

시멘트 바닥에 무릎을 꿇고 앉은 그는 입술이 파랗게 질려 있었다. 하반신이 저려 오고 옆구리가 쑤신다. 이

Hmph. The son of that pro-Jap Yi Inguk got in where even the survivors of revolutionaries find it difficult! Just wait and see!

Full of hope, he crowed to himself, beaming with high spirits.

The Korean War broke out the following year.

The flow of reassuring letters from his son was cut off by the upheaval, leaving a silence that continued until the January Retreat. Yi Inguk, M.D., feared that the cause of his wife's death lay ultimately in the melancholy with which she had watched her only son being sent into the jaws of death.

He carefully read every last word of the newspaper dispatch. But there wasn't any reference to his son's case.

What's that kid dragging his feet for? Can't he get in with these people? When the times are changing, you've got to keep your eyes open and take the initiative. That featherhead!

He folded up the paper and rolled it tightly in his hands.

They say that dragons appear even from creeks, but this boy can't keep up with his old dad.

He clucked with disapproval.

He probably doesn't even know that the family has al-

것만으로도 자기의 생애를 통한 가장 큰 고역이라고 그는 생각하고 있다. 그러나 그것보다는 앞으로 닥쳐올 예기할 수 없는 사태가 공포 속에 그를 휘몰았다.

지나가고 지나오는 구둣발 소리와 목덜미에 퍼부어지는 욕설을 들으면서 꺾이듯이 축 늘어진 그의 머리는 들릴 줄을 몰랐다.

시간만이 흘러가고 있었다.

그의 머릿속에는 짓눌렸던 생각들이 하나씩 꼬리를 치켜들기 시작했다.

'이럴 줄 알았더라면 어디든지 가 숨거나, 진작 남으로라도 도피했을걸……. 그러나 이 판국에 나를 감싸 줄 사람이 어디 있담. 의지할 만한 곳은 다 나와 같은 코스를 밟았거나 조만간에 밟을 사람들이 아닌가. 일본인! 가장 믿었던 성벽이 다 무너지고 난 지금 누구를…….'

'그래도 어떻게 되겠지…….'

이 막연한 기대는 절박한 이 순간에도 그에게서 완전히 떠나버리지는 않았다.

'다행이다. 인민재판의 첫코에 걸리지 않은 것만 해도. 끌려간 사람들의 행방은 전연 알 길이 없다. 즉결 처

ready defected to the south and is himself just hesitating. But news should have gotten that far by now—the meaning of our silence should have gotten through. He's always been too stupid and honest for his own good.

As he got out of the car he spat thickly on the pavement.

Doktor Ri, I will take the responsibility, I give you my guarantee. Send your son to study in our fatherland, the Soviet Union!

Yi Inguk, M.C., could almost hear Stenkov's voice reverberating against his eardrums.

It was the day after the Self-defense Corps became the Public Security Corps. Yi Inguk, M.D., had been taken into custody.

He knelt on the concrete floor—lips blue, legs numb, sides aching. This seemed to him the most painful experience he had yet endured in his life. But even worse, he was swept with fear of an approaching, unpredictable future. As he listened to the footsteps coming and going and to the torrents of abuse being heaped on him, it was beyond his power to lift his head, which drooped like a broken flower.

As time passed, thoughts he had forcibly sup-

형을 당하였다는 소문도 떠돈다. 사흘의 여유만 더 있었더라면 나는 이미 이곳을 떴을는지도 모른다. 다 운명이다. 아니 그래도 무슨 수가 있겠지…….'

"쪽발이 끄나풀, 야 이 새끼야."

고함 소리에 놀라 이인국 박사는 흠칫 머리를 들었다.

때도 묻지 않은 일본 병사 군복에 완장을 찬 젊은이가 쏘아보고 있다. 춘석이다.

이인국 박사는 다시 쳐다볼 힘도 없었다. 모든 사태는 짐작되었다.

이제는 죽는구나, 그는 입 속으로 뇌까렸다.

"왜놈의 밑바시,[16] 이 개새끼야."

일본 군용화가 그의 옆구리를 들이찬다.

"이 새끼, 어디 죽어 봐라."

구둣발은 앞뒤를 가리지 않고 전신을 내지른다.

등골 척수에 다급한 충격을 받자 이인국 박사는 비명을 지르고 꼬꾸라졌다.

그는 현기증을 일으켰다. 어깻죽지를 끌어 바로 앉혀도 몸을 가누지 못하고 한쪽으로 쓰러졌다.

"민족과 조국을 팔아먹은 이 개돼지 같은 놈아, 너는 총살이야, 총살……."

pressed began to creep back into his mind, one by one.

If I had only known it would be like this, I could have hidden somewhere or fled to the south right off. Who can help me now? Anyone who could protect me must be in the same boat or soon will be. The Japanese! That fortress I staked so much on has crumbled and left me defenseless. All the same, something might turn up.

That vague sense of hope had not wholly deserted him even at this crucial moment.

I was lucky at least not to have been caught up in the first round of people's trials. No one seems to know anything about what happens to the ones who are taken away. They say they're judged and executed on the spot. Three more days and I might well have left the city. But in the end it's all a matter of fate. No, not all. There ought to be some way—

"Hey you, Jap-lover! Lackey... ass-kisser!"

Startled by the sudden shouts, Yi Inguk, M.D., raised his head defensively. A youth in a spotless Japanese army uniform with an armband on the sleeve stood glaring down at him. It was Ch'unsŏk. Yi Inguk, M.D., hadn't the strength to stare back. He could guess it all now. "This is the end for me," he murmured to himself.

어렴풋이 꿈속에서처럼 들려왔다. 그러나 그에게는 그 말도 아무런 반향을 일으키지 못했다.

시간이 얼마나 흘렀을까, 자기 앞자락에서 부스럭거리는 감촉과 금속성의 부닥거리는 소리를 듣고 어렴풋이 정신을 차렸다.

노란 털이 엉성한 손목이 시곗줄을 끄르고 있다. 그는 반사적으로 앞자락의 시계 주머니를 부둥켜 쥐면서 손의 임자를 힐끔 쳐다보았다. 눈동자가 파란 중대가리 소년병사가 시곗줄을 거머쥔 채 이빨을 드러내고 히죽이 웃고 있다.

그는 두 손으로 있는 힘을 다해 양복 안주머니를 감싸 쥐었다.

"홍…… 야뽄스끼……."

병사의 눈동자는 점점 노기를 띠어갔다.

"아니, 이것만은!"

그들의 대화는 서로 통하지 않는 대로 손아귀와 눈동자의 대결은 그대로 지속되고 있다.

병사는 뒷박만 한 손으로 이인국 박사의 손을 뿌리치면서 시계를 채어냈다. 시곗줄은 끊어져 고리가 달린 끝머리가 이인국 박사의 손가락 끝에서 달랑거렸다.

"You doormat, son of a bitch!"

A Japanese army boot caught him in the ribs.

"Let's watch you die, dog."

Kicks landed all over his body, front and back alike. As an abrupt shock hit his spinal cord, Yi Inguk, M.D., collapsed with a scream of pain. He slipped into a stupor. He was hauled into a sitting position by somebody pulling at his shoulders but was unable to control his own body and fell over sideways.

"You pig! A bastard like you who sells out his own people and fatherland deserves to die in front of a firing squad. A firing squad!"

The voice sounded faint, as if it were deep within a dream. He could manage no response to the words.

More time seemed to have passed. He became aware of a rustling sound in the front of his clothing and could hear a light metallic tinkle as he began to regain consciousness.

A hand covered with yellow hair was pulling at his watch chain. He instinctively grabbed for his watch pocket and stole a look up at the owner of the hand. It was a blue-eyed, closely cropped Russian soldier with a toothy, sheepish grin. The watch chain was in his hand. The doctor closed his hands

병사는 밖으로 나가버렸다.

'죽음과 시계······.'

이인국 박사는 토막 난 푸념을 되풀이하고 있다.

양쪽 팔목에 팔뚝시계를 둘씩이나 차고도 또 만족이 안 가 자기의 회중시계까지 앗아 가는 그 병정의 모습을 머릿속에 똑똑히 되새겨갈 뿐이다.

감방 속은 빼곡이 찼다.

그러나 고참자와 신입자의 서열은 분명했다. 달포가 지나는 사이에 맨 안쪽 똥통 위에 자리 잡았던 이인국 박사는 삼분지 이의 지점으로 점차 승격되었다.

그는 하루 종일 말이 없었다. 범인 속에 섞여 있던 감방 밀정이 출감된 다음 날부터 불평만을 늘어놓던 축들이 불려 나가 반송장이 되어 들어왔지만, 또 하루 이틀이 지나자 감방 속의 분위기는 여전히 불평과 음식 이야기로 소일되었다.

이인국 박사는 자기의 죄상이라는 것을 폭로하기도 싫었지만 예전에 고등계 형사들에게 실컷 얻어들은 지식이 약이 되어 함구령이 지상 명령이라는 신념을 일관하고 있었다.

with all his strength over the watch pocket of his European-style suit.

"Urgh. Yaponski!"

Anger began to show in the soldier's eyes.

"No, anything but my watch!"

But neither could understand the other, and their confrontation was only one of eye and hand. With a hand as large as a water scoop, the soldier flung Dr. Yi Inguk's arms aside and jerked the watch free. The chain broke and hung dangling from Dr. Yi Inguk's fingers—with only a large open ring at its end. The soldier went out.

Death and a watch.

Yi Inguk, M.D., repeated his lament over and over. He could only lie there calling forth again and again the picture of that soldier—not satisfied with the two watches on each of his wrists, he had to snatch away a pocket watch as well!

As packed as the prison cell was, the system of seniority by which old-timers outranked more recent arrivals was quite clear. Within about a month's time, Yi Inguk, M.D., had been gradually promoted from his original place over the toilet deep within the cell to a position two-thirds of the way up the

그는 간밤에 출감한 학생이 내던지고 간 노어(露語) 회화책을 첫 장부터 곰곰이 뒤지고 있을 뿐이다.

등골이 쏘고 옆구리가 결려온다. 이것으로 고질이 되는가 하는 생각이 없지 않다. 아침저녁으로 기온이 사뭇 내려가고 있다. 아무리 체념한다면서도 초조감을 막을 길 없다.

노어 책을 읽으면서도 그의 청각은 늘 감방 속의 이야기를 놓치지 않고 있다. 그들이 예측하는 식대로의 중형으로 치른다면 자기의 죄상은 너무도 어마어마하다. 양곡조합의 쌀을 몰래 팔아먹은 것이 7년, 양민을 강제로 보국대에 동원했다는 것이 10년, 감정적인 즉결이 아니라 법에 의한 처단이라고 내대지만 이 난리 판국에 법이고 뭣이고 있을까, 마음에만 거슬리면 총살일 판인데…….

'친일파, 민족 반역자, 반일 투사 치료 거부, 일제의 간첩 행위…….'

이건 너무도 어마어마한 죄상이다. 취조할 때 나열하던 그대로 한다면 고작해야 무기징역, 사형감일지도 모른다.

그는 방 안을 둘러보며 후 큰숨을 내쉬었다.

seating order.

He spent his days in silence. The day after an informer among them had been released, the noisiest complainers in the cell were called out and then later sent back half dead. But when only one or two days more had passed, the atmosphere of the cell had returned to normal—complaining about prison and talking about food were the favorite pastimes.

But Yi Inguk, M.D., said nothing. Though, of course, he disliked divulging the details of his crime, he was heeding the advice given him in the old days by an informative acquaintance in the Japanese secret police that silence is the first commandment. He just spent his time diligently studying a Russian conversation book left behind by a student who had been released one night.

He often felt a stinging sensation up and down his back, and his sides were painfully stiff, a condition, he feared, that could easily turn chronic. The temperature in the mornings and evenings would drop extremely low. No matter how he tried to resign himself to these conditions, he could not suppress a feeling of anxiety over his health.

Even while studying his Russian conversation book, he listened carefully to the talk that went on

처마 밑에 바싹 달라붙은 환기창에서 들이비치던 손수건만 한 햇살이 참대자처럼 길어졌다가 실오리만큼 가늘게 떨리며 사라졌다. 그 창살을 거쳐 아득히 보이는 가을 하늘이, 잊었던 지난 일을 한 덩어리로 얽어 휘몰아 오곤 했다. 가슴이 찌릿했다.

밖의 세계와는 영원한 단절이다.

그는 눈을 감았다. 마누라, 아들, 혜숙이, 누구누구…… 그러다가 외과계의 원로 이인국 박사에 이르자, 목구멍이 타는 것같이 꽉 막혔다.

그는 헛기침을 하고 침을 삼켰다.

'그럼, 어쩐단 말이야, 식민지 백성이 별수 있었어. 날구뛴들 소용이 있었느냐 말이야. 어느 놈은 일본 놈한테 아첨을 안 했어. 주는 떡을 안 먹는 놈이 바보지. 흥, 다 그놈이 그놈이었지.'

이인국 박사는 자기변명을 합리화시키고 나면 가슴이 좀 후련해 왔다.

거기다 어저께의 최종 취조 장면에서 얻은 소련 고문관의 표정은 그에게 일루의 희망을 던져주는 것이 있었다. 물론 그것이 억지의 자위(自慰)일지도 모른다고 생각되었지만.

every day inside the cell, never missing a word. Judging from what the others were regarding as heavy penalties for their cases, his crimes loomed monstrous in comparison. Secretly selling rice from a grain cooperative, seven years; pressing innocent citizens into the National Service Corps, ten years. They claimed their trials would lead not to emotional snap decisions but to judgments based on law. Still, what was law in these days of chaos? A momentary lapse could lead to the firing squad.

Pro-Japanese clique, betrayer of the people, refused treatment to anti-Japanese fighter, spied for Japanese imperialists.

These crimes were enormous. If judged and sentenced on all the counts they had listed against him during the investigation, he could easily get life imprisonment or even the death penalty.

He looked around the cell and heaved a long sigh.

In through a ventilating window just under the eaves fell a patch of sunlight no larger than a handkerchief. It lengthened into something like a bamboo measuring stick but soon thinned into a thread and quickly disappeared. The distant autumn sky he could see through the latticework of the vent brought back a host of forgotten memories. They stabbed

아마 스텐코프 소좌라고 했지. 그 혹부리 장교. 직업이 의사라고 했을 때, 독또오루 하고 고개를 기웃거리던 순간의 표정, 그것이 무슨 기적의 예시 같기만 했다.

이인국 박사는 신음 소리에 놀라 눈을 떴다.

복도에 켜 있는 엷은 전등불 빛이 쇠창살을 거쳐 방 안에 줄무늬를 놓으며 비쳐 들어왔다. 그는 환기창 쪽을 올려다보았다. 아직도 동도 트지 않은 깜깜한 밤이다.

생똥 냄새가 코를 찌른다. 바짓가랑이 한쪽이 축축하다. 만져본 손을 코에 갖다 댔다. 구역질이 난다. 역시 똥냄새다.

옆에 누운 청년의 앓는 소리는 계속되고 있다. 찬찬히 눈여겨보았다. 청년 궁둥이도 젖어 있다.

'설산가 부다.'

그는 살창문을 흔들며 교화소원을 고함쳐 불렀다.

"뭐야!"

자다가 깬 듯한 흐린 소리가 들려 왔다.

"환자가…… 이거, 이거 봐요."

창살 사이로 들여다보는 소원의 얼굴은 역광 속에서

at his heart.

An eternal separation from the outside world. He closed his eyes. His wife, son, daughter, Hyesuk... And when he came to the person of Yi Inguk, M.D., acknowledged authority in the field of surgery, he choked, his throat burning. He coughed dryly and swallowed.

What do they expect of a person, anyway? There's no other way out for the people of a colony. They had no place for you, no matter what your talent. Who didn't cater to the Japs at one time or another? Only a fool rejects the proffered cake. None of us is clean.

Now that Yi Inguk, M.D., had rationalized his behavior and vindicated himself a bit, he felt a sense of relief.

What's more, there was something he had caught in the expression on the face of a Russian adviser at his final interrogation two days earlier, something that offered a straw of hope. Of course, he couldn't be sure he wasn't fooling himself out of desperation.

What did they call the man? Something like Major Stenkov. The one with the wen on his face who peered across for a moment with that expression on his face as he repeated *"Doktor, Doktor,"* when

챙 붙은 모자 밑의 둥그스름한 윤곽밖에 알려지지 않는다.

이인국 박사는 청년의 궁둥이께를 손가락으로 가리키며 들여다보고 있다.

"이거, 피로군, 피야."

그는 그제야 붉은빛을 발견하고 놀란 소리를 쳤다.

"적리[17]야, 이질……."

그는 직업의식에서 떠오르는 대로 큰 소리를 질렀다.

"뭐, 적리?"

바깥 소리는 확실히 납득이 안 간 음성이다.

"피똥 쌌소, 피똥을…… 이것 봐요."

그는 언성을 더욱 높였다.

"응, 피똥……."

아우성 소리에 감방 안의 사람들은 하나 둘 눈을 뜨며 저마다 놀란 소리를 쳤다.

"적리, 이거 전염병이요, 전염병."

"뭐 전염병……."

그제야 교화소원이 문을 열고 들어왔다.

얼마 후 환자는 격리되었고 남은 사람들은 똥을 닦느라고 한참 법석을 치고 다시 잠을 불러일으키질 못했

the matter of occupation had been clarified. It seemed to presage a miracle of some sort.

Yi Inguk, M.D., opened his eyes with a start at the sound of moaning next to him.

The thin glow of the hallway light fell through the iron bars and cast a striped pattern across the interior of the cell. He looked up toward the ventilating window. It was still black outside, well before daybreak.

The stench of fresh excrement stabbed at his nostrils. One leg of his trousers felt damp. He touched the wetness and lifted his fingers to his nose. Definitely excrement. He was nauseated. It had come from the young man next to him, who continued to groan in pain. He took a long, careful look at the youth. His buttocks were thoroughly soaked.

Looks like diarrhea.

He rattled the barred door and shouted for one of the guards.

"What do you want!"

He could hear the thick voice of a guard just aroused from his sleep.

"Something's wrong with this man... Look—come take a look!"

다.

이튿날 미결감 다른 감방에서 또 같은 증세의 환자가 두셋 발생했다. 날이 갈수록 환자는 늘기만 했다.

이 판국에 병만 나면 열의 아홉은 죽는 길밖에 없다고 생각한 이인국 박사는 새로운 위협에 사로잡히기 시작했다.

저녁 후 이인국 박사는 고문관실로 불려 나갔다.

"동무는 당분간 환자의 응급 치료실에서 일하시오."

이게 무슨 청천벽력 같은 기적일까, 그는 통역의 말을 의심했다.

소련 장교와 통역관을 번갈아 쳐다보는 그의 눈동자는 생기를 띠어갔다.

"알겠소, 엥……?"

"네."

다짐에 따라 이인국 박사는 기쁨을 억지로 감추며 평범한 어조로 대답했다.

'글쎄 하늘이 무너져도 솟아날 구멍은 있다니까.'

그는 아무 표정도 나타내지 않으려고 이를 악물었다.

죽어 넘어진 송장이 개 치우듯 꾸려져 나가는 것을

As the guard looked in between the bars, his face was nothing but a roundish outline, topped by a cap and brim, against the light. Yi Inguk, M.D., had pointed in the general direction of the youth's buttocks and was now studying his raised fingers.

"This is blood. Blood!"

He had only now discovered the redness on his fingers and was crying out in surprise.

"He's passing blood. This boy's got dysentery!"

His loud voice carried the confidence of his professional knowledge.

"What? Dysentery?"

The voice outside didn't sound fully convinced yet.

"He's passed blood in his stool. Bloody diarrhea... Take a look, here."

His voice climbed in pitch.

"Hmm. Bloody, you say..."

At the shouting, other inmates opened their eyes one by one and added their startled cries to the din.

"Dysentery. It's contagious. Dysentery's a contagious disease."

"What, contagious?"

The guard finally opened the door and came into

보고 이인국 박사는 꼭 자기 일같이만 느껴졌다.

"의사, 이것은 나의 천직이다."

그는 몇 번이고 감격에 차 중얼거렸다. 그는 있는 힘을 다해 자기 담당의 환자를 치료했다. 이러한 일은 그의 실력이 혹부리 고문관의 유다른 관심을 끌게 한 계기를 만들어 주었다.

사상범을 옥사시키는 경우 책임자에게 큰 문책이 온다는 것은 훨씬 후에야 그가 안 일이다.

소련 군의관에게 기술이 인정된 이인국 박사는 계속 병원에 근무하게 되었다. 그러나 죄상 처벌의 결말에 대하여는 알 길이 없었다.

그는 이 절호의 기회를 최대한으로 활용하고 싶었다. 이제는 죽어도 한이 없을 것만 같았다.

어떻게 하여 이 보이지 않는 구속에서까지 완전히 벗어날 수는 없을까.

그는 환자의 치료를 하면서도 늘 스텐코프의 왼쪽 뺨에 붙은 오리알만 한 혹을 생각하고 있었다.

불구라면 불구로 볼 수 있는 그 혹을 가지고 고급 장교에까지 승진했다는 것은 소위 말하는 당성(黨性)이 강하거나 그렇지 않으면 전공(戰功)이 특별했음에 틀림

the cell.

The patient was removed a while later, and the inmates raised such a ruckus trying to scrub away the mess that they were unable to get back to sleep again.

Two days later, two or three cases showing the same symptoms were discovered in another cell. As the days passed, the number of victims seemed only to increase. Yi Inguk, M.D., felt himself in the grip of a new menace. In these conditions, he estimated, nine out of ten would die if they caught the disease.

After supper, Yi Inguk, M.D., was called to the adviser's office.

"Comrade, for the time being you will treat patients in the first-aid room."

What sort of miracle was this? Like lightning from a clear sky. He doubted the interpreter's words. His eyes lit up as he stared first at the Russian officer, then at the interpreter, and back again.

"Do you understand?"

"Yes, sir."

Yi Inguk, M.D., struggled to mask the elation he felt and managed to answer with composure.

Like I say. The roof may fall in but there's always a way

없다는 생각이 들었다.

그것 하나만 물고 늘어지면 무엇인가 완전히 살아날 틈사구가 생길 것만 같았다.

이인국 박사의 뜨내기 노어도 가끔 순시하는 스텐코프와 인사말을 주고받을 수 있을 정도로 진전되었다.

이 안에서의 모든 독서는 금지되었지만 노어 교본과 당사(黨史)만은 허용되었다.

이인국 박사는 마치 생명의 열쇠나 되는 듯이 초보 노어 책을 거의 암송하다시피 했다.

크리스마스를 전후하여 장교들의 주연이 베풀어지는 기회가 거듭되었다.

얼근히 주기를 띤 스텐코프가 순시를 돌았다.

이인국 박사는 오늘의 이 기회를 놓치지 않겠다고 마음먹었다.

수일 전 소군 장교 한 사람이 급성 맹장염이 터져 복막염으로 번졌다.

그 환자의 실을 뽑는 옆에 온 스텐코프에게 이인국 박사는 말 절반 손짓 절반으로 혹을 수술하겠다는 의사를 표명했다.

스텐코프는 '하라쇼'[18]를 연발했다.

out.

He clenched his teeth to suppress any expression on his face that might betray him.

When Yi Inguk, M.D., saw the corpses being wrapped up and shipped out like so much cordwood, he felt as if it were his own doing. "Medicine is my mission in life," he would murmur over and over with strong feeling. He threw himself into the work of serving the patients assigned him. And these duties also happened to attract the particular interest of the Russian adviser with the wen on his face.

Not until much later did he finally learn that serious censure awaited those responsible for the death in prison of an ideological criminal like himself.

Yi Inguk, M.D., recognized by the Russian medical officer for his technical skill, was now allowed to continue his duties at the hospital itself. But still he had no knowledge of the final disposition of the criminal charges against him.

He vowed, however, to make the best of this remarkable opportunity. Even death itself could not deter him now. Shouldn't there be some way to work free of the invisible shackles that held him

그 후 몇 번 통역을 사이에 두고 수술 계획에 대한 자세한 의사를 진술할 기회가 생겼다.

이인국 박사는 일본인 시장의 혹을 수술하던 일을 회상하면서 자신 있는 설복을 했다.

'동경 경응대학 병원에서도 못 하겠다는 것을 내가 거뜬히 해치우지 않았던가.'

그는 혼자 머릿속에서 자문자답하면서 이번 일에 도박 같은 심정으로 생명을 걸었다.

소련 군의관을 입회시키고 몇 차례의 예비 진단이 치러졌다.

수술일은 왔다.

이인국 박사는 손에 익은 자기 병원의 의료 기재를 전부 운반하여 오게 했다.

군의관 세 사람이 보조하기로 했지만 집도는 이인국 박사 자신이 했다. 야전 병원의 젊은 군의관들이란 그에게 있어선 한갓 풋내기로밖에 보이지 않았다.

그는 수술을 진행하는 동안 그들 군의관들을 자기 집 조수 부리듯 했다. 집도 이후의 수술대는 완전히 자기 전단하의 왕국이라고 생각되었다.

그러나 아까 수술 직전에 사인한, 실패되는 경우에는

here?

While he treated his patients each day, his only thought was of the duck-egg-sized wen on Stenkov's left cheek. With such a deformity—for one could call it that, he thought—how could Stenkov have risen to such high rank without some powerful influence in the Party or particular heroism on the battlefield? No doubt about it. It seemed he would gain salvation if only he sank his teeth into that wen and hung on for dear life.

Yi Inguk, M.D., had progressed in his Russian to the point where he could exchange halting pleasantries when Stenkov came by on his occasional rounds. Though reading matter was generally prohibited here, Russian-language texts and Party histories were allowed as exceptions. Yi Inguk, M.D., nearly memorized his Russian primer, as if it were the key to his very life.

Several opportunities presented themselves around Christmas time, when the officers were having their holiday celebrations. A slightly tipsy Stenkov came by on his rounds. This time, Yi Inguk, M.D., promised himself, he would not miss his chance.

Several days before, a Russian officer had been

총살에 처한다는 서약서가 통일된 정신을 순간순간 흐려놓곤 한다.

수술대에 누운 스텐코프의 침착하면서도 긴장에 찼던 얼굴, 그것도 전신 마취가 끝난 후 삼 분이 못 갔다.

간호부는 가제[19]로 이인국 박사의 이마에 내맺힌 땀방울을 연방 찍어내고 있다.

기구가 부딪는 금속성과 서로의 숨소리만이 고촉의 반사등이 내리비치는 방 안의 질식할 것 같은 침묵을 헤실[20] 짓고 있다.

수술은 예상 이상의 단시간으로 끝났다.

위생복을 벗은 이인국 박사의 전신은 땀으로 흠뻑 젖었다.

완치되어 퇴원하는 날 스텐코프는 이인국 박사의 손을 부서져라 쥐면서 외쳤다.

"꺼삐딴 리, 스바씨보."[21]

이인국 박사는 입을 헤벌리고 웃기만 했다. 마음의 감옥에서 해방된 것만 같았다.

"아진, 아진……[22] 오첸 하라쇼."[23]

스텐코프는 엄지손가락을 높이 들면서 네가 첫째라

hospitalized with acute appendicitis complicated by peritonitis. Stenkov came up beside Yi Inguk, M.D., as he was removing the stitches from his patient. He turned to the major and proposed, half in words and half in gesture, that he operate to remove the wen.

Stenkov responded enthusiastically with a volley of *khorosho's*.

After that, he had a number of occasions to present his opinions in detail on the proposed surgery when they talked it over through an interpreter. Yi Inguk, M.D., was persuasively reassuring as he spoke confidently of having removed a wen for the Japanese mayor.

Didn't I lop that wen off neat as you please, even after Keio University Hospital said it couldn't be done?

Silently asking and answering his own questions as he went along, he prepared, with a gambler's heart, to stake his life on this one opportunity.

The Russian medical officer was brought in for consultation, and they conducted a number of preparatory examinations.

The day of the operation arrived. Yi Inguk, M.D., had them bring in all his own surgical equipment, with which his touch was sure.

는 듯이 이인국 박사의 어깨를 치며 찬양했다.

다음 날 스텐코프는 이인국 박사를 자기 방으로 불렀다.

그가 이인국 박사에게 스스로 손을 내밀어 예절적인 악수를 청한 것은 이것이 처음이었다.

'적과 적이 맞부딪치면서 이렇게 백팔십도로 전환될 수가 있을까, 노랑 대가리도 역시 본심에서는 하나의 인간임에는 틀림없는 것이 아닌가.'

"내일부터는 집에서 통근해도 좋소."

이인국 박사는 막혔던 둑이 터지는 것 같은 큰숨을 삼켜가면서 내쉬었다.

이번에는 이인국 박사가 스텐코프의 손을 잡았다.

"스바씨보, 스바씨보."

"혹 나한테 무슨 부탁이 없소?"

이인국 박사는 문득 시계가 머리에 떠올랐다.

그러면서도 곧이어 이 마당에 그런 이야기를 꺼낸다는 것은 오히려 꾀죄죄하게 보이지 않을까 하는 생각이 뒤따랐다. 그러나 아무래도 그 미련이 가셔지지 않았다.

이인국 박사는 비록 찾지 못하는 경우가 있더라도 솔직히 심중을 털어놓으리라고 마음먹었다.

Though three medical officers assisted him, it was Yi Inguk, M.D., himself who held the scalpel. These young field hospital doctors were no more than novices to him. In the course of the operation, he used them as he had used the assistants in his own hospital. The thought came to him that once the incision had been made the operating room became his absolute kingdom.

From time to time, however, the fact of the pledge signed just before the operation invaded his thoughts. In the case of failure, he would accept the firing squad.

Stenkov lay on the operating table looking tense though composed. It was not yet three minutes since the hypodermic needle, full of anesthetic, had pierced his spine.

The nurse continued to wipe away with a wad of gauze the drops of sweat that formed on Dr. Yi Inguk's forehead. Only the metallic clink of instruments and the sound of breathing cut through the oppressive silence of the room, which was illuminated by the rays of an intense overhead reflector light.

The operation was over sooner than anticipated. When Yi Inguk, M.D., removed his operating gown,

그는 통역의 보조를 받아가며 시간과 장소를 정확히 회상하면서 시계를 약탈당한 경위를 상세히 설명했다.

스텐코프는 혹이 붙었던 뺨을 쓰다듬으면서 긴장된 모습으로 듣고 있었다.

"염려 없소, 독또오루 리, 위대한 붉은 군대가 그럴 리가 없소. 만약 있었다 하더라도 그것은 무슨 착각이었을 것이오. 내가 책임지고 찾도록 하겠소."

스텐코프의 얼굴에 결의를 띤 심각한 표정이 스쳐가는 것을 이인국 박사는 똑바로 쳐다보았다.

'공연한 말을 끄집어내어 일껏 잘 되어 가는 일에 부스럼을 만드는 것은 아닐까.'

그는 솟구치는 불안과 후회를 짓눌렀다.

"안심하시오, 독또오루 리, 하하하."

스텐코프는 큰 웃음으로 넌지시 말끝을 막았다.

이인국 박사는 죽음의 직전에서 풀려나 집으로 향했다.

어느 사이에 저렇게 노어로 의사 표시를 할 수 있게 되었느냐고 스텐코프가 감탄하더라는 통역의 말을 되뇌면서……

his entire body was drenched with sweat.

On the day his recovery was complete and he was released from the hospital, Stenkov took Dr. Yi Inguk's hand in his crushing grip and roared as he squeezed.

"Kapitan Ri, *spasibo!*"

Dr. Yi Inguk's mouth fell open and he could only laugh. It was as if he had been released from a spiritual prison.

"*Ochen, ocheno... Ochen khorosho!*"

Stenkov gave a thumbs-up gesture to express his high regard for Yi Inguk, M.D., and clapped him on the shoulder as a sign of praise.

The following day Stenkov called Yi Inguk, M.D., to his room. He offered his hand to the doctor in the first formal gesture of real courtesy he had shown him.

Can one confront one's enemy and manage such a complete conversion as this? Maybe even these yellow-tops are human, too, at heart.

"Starting tomorrow you may commute to work from your home."

Yi Inguk, M.D., gulped and sighed like a chimney that had just come unblocked. This time it was he

차가 브라운 씨의 관사 앞에 닿았다.

성조기(星條旗)를 보면서 이인국 박사는 그날의 적기(赤旗)와 돌려온 시계를 생각했다.

응접실에 안내된 이인국 박사는 주인이 나오기를 기다리면서 방 안을 둘러보았다. 대사관으로는 여러 번 찾아갔지만 집으로 찾아온 것은 이번이 처음이다.

삼 년 전 딸이 미국으로 갈 때부터 신세 진 사람이다.

벽 쪽 책꽂이에는 『이조실록(李朝實錄)』 『대동야승(大東野乘)』 등 한적(漢籍)이 빼곡이 차 있고 한쪽에는 고서(古書)의 질책(帙冊)[24]이 가지런히 쌓여져 있다.

맞은편 책장 위에는 작은 금동불상(金銅佛像) 곁에 몇 개의 골동품이 진열되어 있다. 십이 폭 예서(隸書) 병풍 앞 탁자 위에 놓인 재떨이도 세월의 때 묻은 백자기다.

저것들도 다 누군가가 가져다준 것이 아닐까 하는 데 생각이 미치자 이인국 박사는 얼굴이 화끈해졌다.

그는 자기가 들고 온 상감진사(象嵌辰砂) 고려청자 화병에 눈길을 돌렸다. 사실 그것을 내놓는 데는 얼마간의 아쉬움이 없지 않았다. 국외로 내어 보낸다는 자책감 같은 것은 아예 생각해 본 일이 없는 그였다.

차라리 이인국 박사에게는, 저렇게 많으니 무엇이 그

who grasped Stenkov's hand.

"Spasibo! Spasibo!"

"But don't you perhaps have anything to ask of me? A favor, maybe?"

Yi Inguk, M.D., suddenly thought of his watch. But then he hesitated for fear that dragging that story in so abruptly here and now would actually seem rather shabby. Still, no matter what, he'd never lose his feelings for that watch. Yi Inguk, M.D., decided to reveal honestly all he felt about the watch even though there might be no chance of recovering it.

With the aid of an interpreter, he established what he could of the time and place and gave all the details he could recall of the theft. Stenkov listened tensely as he fingered the spot on his cheek where the wen had once been.

"Nothing to worry about, Doktor Ri. We do not condone such things in the Great Red Army. And even if something like that happened, it could only have been a misunderstanding of some sort. I will take responsibility and see that you recover your watch."

Yi Inguk, M.D., who was watching Stenkov close-ly, saw a serious and determined expression cross

리 소중하고 달갑게 여겨지겠느냐는 망설임이 더 앞섰다.

브라운 씨가 나오자 이인국 박사는 웃으며 선물을 내어놓았다. 포장을 풀고 난 브라운 씨는 만면에 미소를 띠며 기쁨을 참지 못하는 듯 댕큐를 거듭 부르짖었다.

"참 이거 귀중한 것입니다."

"뭐 대단한 것이 아닙니다만 그저 제 성의입니다."

이인국 박사는 안도감에 잇닿는 만족을 느끼면서 브라운 씨의 기쁨에 맞장구를 쳤다.

브라운 씨의 영어 반 한국말 반으로 섞어 하는 이야기를 들으면서 이인국 박사는 흐뭇한 기분에 젖었다.

"닥터 리는 영어를 어디서 배웠습니까?"

"일제시대에 일본말 식으로 배웠지요. 예를 들면 '잣도 이즈 아 캣도' 식으루요."

"그런데 지금 발음은 좋은데요. 문법이 아주 정확한 스탠더드 잉글리시입니다."

그는 이 말을 들을 때 문득 스텐코프의 말이 연상됐다. 그러고 보면 영국에 조상을 가졌다는 브라운 씨는 아르(R) 발음을 그렇게 나타내지 않는 것 같게 여겨졌다.

his face.

Have I blundered by bringing up this needless business, just when everything was going so well?

He tried to suppress the hidden feelings of misgiving and regret.

"Rest assured, Doctor Ri... ha, ha, ha."

Stenkov interrupted himself with his own booming laughter, leaving his implication in the air.

Yi Inguk, M.D., had been rescued from the brink of death and was headed home. He could still hear the interpreter relating Stenkov's exclamation.

Where did he ever learn to express himself like that in Russian?

The car pulled up in front of Mr. Brown's residence. The sight of the Stars and Stripes made Yi Inguk, M.D., think of the red flag he had received along with his watch the day it was returned.

Yi Inguk, M.D., was shown into the living room, and he had time to look around while he waited for his host to appear. Though he had called on Mr. Brown a number of times at the embassy, this was his first visit to the man's home.

His indebtedness dated back three years, to when his daughter had gone to the United States.

"얼마 전부터 개인 교수를 받고 있습니다."

"아, 그렇습니까."

이인국 박사는 자기의 어학적 재질에 은근히 자긍을 느꼈다.

브라운 씨가 부엌 쪽으로 갔다 오더니 양주 몇 병이 놓인 쟁반이 따라 나왔다.

"아무 거라도 마음에 드는 것으로 하십시오."

이인국 박사는 보드카 잔을 신통한 안주도 없이 억지로라도 단숨에 들이켜야 목 시원해하던 스텐코프를 브라운 씨 얼굴에 겹쳐보고 있다.

그는 혈압 때문에 술을 조절해야 하는 자기 체질에 알맞게 스카치 잔을 핥듯이 조금씩 목을 축이면서 브라운 씨의 이야기를 기다렸다.

"그거, 국무성에서 통지 왔습니다."

이인국 박사는 뛸 듯이 기뻤으나 솟구치는 흥분을 억제하면서 천천히 손을 내밀어 악수를 청했다.

"댕큐, 댕큐."

어쩌면 이것은 수술 후의 스텐코프가 자기에게 하던 방식 그대로인지도 모른다는 생각이 들었다.

이인국 박사는 지성이면 감천이라구, 나의 처세법은

The bookcase along one wall was jammed with Korean historical works written in Chinese, such as the *Veritable Records of the Yi Dynasty* and the *Taedong Compendium of Private Histories*. The bookcase across the room held neatly wrapped sets of classic texts. On a desk, around a small gilt-bronze Buddha, a number of antique curios were grouped for display. In front of a twelvefold screen of ancient Chinese calligraphy stood a small wine table on which rested a patina-filmed white porcelain bowl, serving here as an ashtray.

All of these must have been gifts brought by various callers. Yi Inguk, M.D., felt his face suddenly flush at the thought of the Koryŏ inlaid celadon vase he had brought. Actually, he was giving it up with some reluctance. He really hadn't thought it reprehensible to send these things out of the country. Rather, Dr. Yi Inguk's main question was why a man would want so many of these things. Where was the value, the satisfaction, in having them?

As soon as Mr. Brown came in, Yi Inguk, M.D., presented his gift with a smile. When Mr. Brown had unwrapped the parcel a smile spread across his face, too. He thanked the doctor over and over, unable to conceal his pleasure.

유에스에이에도 통하는구나 하는 기고만장한 기분이었다.

청자 병을 몇 번이고 쓰다듬으면서 술잔을 거듭하는 브라운 씨도 몹시 즐거운 기분이었다.

"미국에 가서의 모든 일도 잘 부탁합니다."

"네, 염려 마십시오. 떠나실 때 소개장을 써드리지요."

"감사합니다."

"역사는 짧지만, 미국은 지상의 낙토입니다. 양국의 우호와 친선에 도움이 되기를 바랍니다."

"땡큐……."

다음 날 휴전선 지대로 같이 수렵하러 가기로 약속하고 이인국 박사는 브라운 씨 대문을 나섰다.

이번 새로 장만한 영국제 쌍발 엽총의 짙푸른 총신을 머리에 그리면서 그의 몸은 날기라도 할 듯이 두둥실 가벼웠다. 이인국 박사는 아까 수술한 환자의 경과가 궁금했으나 그것은 곧 씻겨져 갔다.

그의 마음속에는 새로운 포부와 희망이 부풀어 올랐다.

신체검사는 이미 끝난 것이고 외무부 출국 수속도 국무성 통지만 오면 즉일 될 수 있게 담당 책임자에게 교

"This is quite a valuable piece, indeed."

"Oh, it's really nothing, just an expression of good-will."

A sense of relief became a flush of satisfaction as Yi Inguk, M.D., joined in Mr. Brown's pleasant mood. As he listened to the American's mixed English and Korean pleasantries, he felt suffused with a warm feeling of accomplishment.

"Dr. Yi, where did you learn your English?"

"I learned it during the Japanese period, in Japanese style. You know, *'Zatto izu ah katto'* for 'That is a cat' and so on."

"But your pronunciation is so good now. And your grammar's quite accurate, too. Standard English."

These words suddenly called to mind what Stenkov had said about his Russian.

It seemed to him that Mr. Brown, who said his ancestors came from England, didn't pronounce his "r" sounds fully.

"I have had a private tutor for some time now."

"Oh, is that so?"

Yi Inguk, M.D., felt a restrained pride in his linguistic abilities.

Mr. Brown disappeared for a moment toward the kitchen and returned with a tray of various foreign

섭이 되어 있지 않은가? 빠르면 일주일 내에 떠나게 될지도 모른다는 브라운 씨의 말이 떠올랐다.

대학을 갓 나와 임상 경험도 신통치 않은 것들이 미국에만 갔다 오면 별이라도 딴 듯이 날치는 꼴이 눈꼴사나웠다.

'어디 나두 댕겨오구 나면 보자!'

문득 딸 나미와 아들 원식의 얼굴이 한꺼번에 망막으로 휘몰아왔다. 그는 두 주먹을 불끈 쥐며 얼굴에 경련을 일으키듯 긴장을 띠다가 어색한 미소를 흘려보냈다.

'흥, 그 사마귀 같은 일본 놈들 틈에서도 살았고, 닥싸귀²⁵⁾ 같은 로스케 속에서도 살아났는데, 양키라고 다를까……. 혁명이 일겠으면 일구, 나라가 바뀌겠으면 바뀌구, 아직 이 이인국의 살 구멍은 막히지 않았다. 나보다 얼마든지 날뛰던 놈들도 있는데, 나쯤이야…….'

그는 허공을 향하여 마음껏 소리치고 싶었다.

'그러면 우선 비행기 회사에 들러 형편이나 알아볼까…….'

이인국 박사는 캘리포니아 특산 시가를 비스듬히 문채 지나가는 택시를 불러 세웠다.

그는 스프링이 튈 듯이 복스²⁶⁾에 털썩 주저앉았다.

liquors.

"Do have whatever you wish."

As Yi Inguk, M.D., looked at Mr. Brown, the American's face was replaced by Stenkov's, who had seemed satisfied only when he could down his vodka in a gulp, not bothering with food on the side. The doctor, whose high blood pressure and general constitution forced him to moderate his drinking, only sipped at his scotch, warming his palate as he waited to hear what Mr. Brown had to say.

"Well, we've received notification from the Department of State."

Yi Inguk, M.D., could have leaped for joy but, subduing the rush of excitement he felt, instead extended his hand to shake Brown's.

"Thank you. Thank you."

It struck him that he was responding just as Stenkov had to him after the operation.

It seems my way of managing the world works even with the Americans, thought Yi Inguk, M.D., in high spirits. *True sincerity can move Heaven itself, they say.*

Mr. Brown, too, seemed particularly pleased as he caressed the celadon vase and refilled his whiskey glass.

"반도호텔로……."

차창을 거쳐 보이는 맑은 가을 하늘은 이인국 박사에

게는 더욱 푸르고 드높게만 느껴졌다.

---

* '까삐딴'은 영어의 Captain에 해당하는 노어(露語)다. 8·15 직
후 소련군이 북한에 진주하자 '까삐딴'이 '우두머리'나 '최고'라
는 뜻으로 많이 쓰였는데, 그 발음이 와전되어 '꺼삐딴'으로 통
용되었다.

1) 지기(知己). 지기지우. 자기의 속마음을 참되게 알아주는 친구.
2) 월삼 십칠석. '월삼'은 미국의 회사 이름 'Waltham'을 뜻하는
   말로, 월샘(Waltham) 사에서 만든 'Waltham 17 Jewel'이라는
   시계를 의미한다.
3) 각모(角帽). 사각모자.
4) 쓰메에리[詰襟]. 깃의 높이가 4cm쯤 되게 하여, 목을 둘러 바
   싹 여미게 지은 양복. 학생복으로 많이 지었다.
5) 기류계(寄留屆). '기류 신고(寄留申告)'의 전 용어로, 예전에 본적
   지 이외의 일정한 곳에 주소나 거소를 두던 일을 관할 관청에
   보고하던 일. 또는 그런 서류.
6) 복재(伏在). 몰래 숨어 있음.
7) 체모(體貌). 체면. 몸차림이나 몸가짐.
8) 혼반(婚班). 서로 혼인을 맺을 만한 양반의 지체.
9) 훈도시[褌]. 남자의 국소를 가리는 데 쓰는 아주 좁고 긴 천.
10) 유카다[浴衣]. 아래위에 걸쳐서 입는, 두루마기 모양의 긴 무
    명 홑옷.
11) 단스. '장롱'을 의미하는 일본어.
12) 로스케. Ruskii. 러시아 사람을 낮잡아 이르는 말.
13) 낫세. '나잇살'의 잘못.
14) 다찌끼리. 조각면. 박스 기사.
15) 독또오루. 닥터.
16) 밑바시. '음식 찌꺼기'를 가리키는 함경도 사투리.
17) 적리(赤痢). 급성 전염병인 이질의 하나. 여름철에 많이 발생
    하며, 입을 통하여 전염하여 2~3일 동안의 잠복기가 지난
    후, 발열과 복통이 따르고 피와 곱이 섞인 대변을 누게 된다.

"I am afraid I shall be asking you many favors concerning my visit to America."

"There's no need to worry about that. I'll write you a letter of introduction before you leave."

"Thank you very much."

"Our history may be short, but America is a wonderful place! I hope your visit will help to promote friendship and goodwill between our two countries."

"Thank you."

After promising to meet the next day for a hunting expedition into the Demilitarized Zone, Yi Inguk, M.D., left Mr. Brown's home. There was a spring in his step as he pictured the deep-blue barrels of his new, double-barreled English hunting rifle. Yi Inguk, M.D., was concerned for a moment over the condition of the patient he had operated on a while before, but that soon passed. New feelings of ambition and hope swelled within his heart.

It had been arranged with the responsible official at the Ministry of Foreign Affairs that, the physical examination now complete, his exit papers would be issued the day he received the State Department notification. He recalled Mr. Brown's comment that he could be leaving within a week's time if all went

세균성 적리와 아메바 적리로 나눈다.

18) 하라쇼. '좋습니다', '알았습니다'의 러시아어.

19) 가제(Gaze). 거즈(gauze). 가볍고 부드러운 무명베. 흔히 붕대로 사용한다.

20) 헤살. 일을 짓궂게 훼방함. 또는 그런 짓.

21) 스바씨보. '고맙소'라는 뜻의 러시아어.

22) 아진. '아주'라는 뜻의 러시아어.

23) 오첸 하라쇼. '참으로 좋소'라는 뜻의 러시아어.

24) 질책(帙冊). 여러 권으로 한 벌을 이루는 책.

25) 닥싸귀. '도꼬마리'의 함경도 사투리. 국화과의 한해살이풀. 열매에 갈고리 같은 가시가 있어 옷에 잘 붙는다.

26) 복스(box). 무두질한 송아지 가죽.

* 이 책의 한국어판 저작권은 사단법인 한국문예학술저작권협회로부터 저작물의 사용 허락에 대한 동의를 받았다.

* 작가 고유의 문체나 당시 쓰이던 용어를 그대로 살려 원문에 최대한 가깝게 표기하고자 하였다. 단, 현재 쓰이지 않는 말이나 띄어쓰기는 현행 맞춤법에 맞게 표기하였다.

《사상계(思想界)》, 1962

well.

So many people, fresh out of college with no particular clinical experience, carry on in that unseemly way as if they'd plucked themselves a star—all because they'd made a trip to the United States. Well, I'm going this time. Once I get back, we'll see!

Suddenly a vision of his daughter Nami and his son Wŏnshik came to him. He clenched his fists tightly, and his face tensed momentarily as if he were on the brink of a seizure. Then an odd smile passed across his face.

Hmm. I've lived among those warty Japanese, made it out of the grasp of those brutish Russians, and now the Yankees—could they be much different? Revolutions may come and the nation change hands, but the way out has never been blocked for Yi Inguk. There used to be so many who seemed to outdo me from time to time. I've made it through, but what about them?

He wanted to shout his heart out into the void.

Shall I drop by the airline office and look into the ticket situation?

With the custom-made California cigar clamped at a jaunty angle in his teeth, Yi Inguk, M.D., hailed a passing taxi.

"Bando Hotel."

The clear autumn sky outside the car window was bluer and loftier to Yi Inguk, M.D., than others might have realized.

Translated by Marshall R. Pihl

해설

Afterword

역사적 격동기 한 지식인의
굴절된 초상(肖像)

서재길 (문학평론가)

「꺼삐딴 리」는 일제 식민지 시기에서 해방기와 한국 전쟁을 거쳐 냉전체제로 이어지는 역사적 격동기를 배경으로 민족공동체의 운명과 공공선보다는 일신의 출세와 가족의 안위만을 위해 살아온 지식인을 주인공으로 등장시켜 한국 현대사의 질곡이 한 지식인의 내면에 가져온 굴절을 그리고 있는 작품이다.

식민지 시기 제국대학을 졸업한 개업의(開業醫)인 주인공 이인국은 일제 말기 자식들을 일본인 학교에 보냈을 뿐만 아니라 가정에서도 일본어만 쓰게 하여 '국어 상용의 가(家)'라는 칭송을 받을 정도로 철저한 친일파이다. 해방이 되어 소련군이 38선 이북에 진주하게 되

A Refracted Portrait of an Intellectual
in Times of Historical Turmoil

Seo Jae-kil (literary critic)

The short story "Kapitan Ri" depicts how the ordeal of modern Korea distorted the inner world of an intellectual, who only lived for his own success and the safety of his family, rather than paying attention to the fate of the nation or the public good. The story takes place during several decades of turbulent times in Korean history: from the Japanese colonial period through liberation and the Korean War to the period of the Cold War.

Yi Inguk, the protagonist, is a physician in private practice. He graduated from the Imperial University during the Japanese colonial period. He is extremely pro-Japanese in his sympathies, to the point that

자 그는 감옥으로 끌려가 친일파로 단죄될 처지에 놓이게 된다. 그러나 자신이 가진 의사로서의 능력과 감옥에서 속성(速成)으로 익힌 러시아어를 이용하여 소련군 장교에게 환심을 사게 되면서 그는 위기에서 벗어났을 뿐만 아니라 아들을 러시아 유학까지 보내는 수완을 발휘한다. 소설의 제목이기도 한 '꺼삐딴 리'는 바로 이 소련 장교에 의해 붙여진 그의 또다른 이름이기도 하였다. 한국전쟁 발발 후 1·4 후퇴 당시 월남한 그는 서울에 병원을 차리고 권력층과 상류층을 주 고객으로 하는 종합병원의 원장으로 승승장구하지만, 자신의 미국 유학을 주선해 준 미국인 교수와의 결혼을 선언한 딸의 편지를 받고 마음이 심란하다. 그러나 도미(渡美)를 위한 미국 국무성 초청장을 받기 위해 대사관 직원에게 고려 청자를 선물로 바치는 등 그의 탐욕은 그칠 줄을 모른다.

이 작품은 이인국이 미 대사관 직원 브라운과의 약속 시간을 확인하기 위해 시계를 확인하는 장면에서 과거에 대한 회상으로 이어졌다가 마지막에는 브라운에게 고려 청자를 건네 주고 나와서 택시를 타고 반도호텔로 가는 장면에서 끝난다. 이같은 역전적 서사구성은 작가

his family received the "National Language (Japanese) Family" certificate. He not only sent his children to Japanese schools toward the end the colonial period, but also made them use only Japanese, even at home.

After the liberation, when the Soviet army is deployed and stationed in the Korean peninsula north of the 38th parallel, Yi is imprisoned and facing more punishment for his pro-Japanese activities. However, using his skills as a doctor and with the Russian language, which he mastered quickly in prison, he not only avoided the crisis, by currying favor with a Russian officer, but was also able to send his son to study in Russia.

"Kapitan Ri," the story's namesake, was a name Yi was given by the Russian officer. After the Korean War broke out, Yi defected to South Korea during the January Retreat. In Seoul, he founded a private hospital, whose main clientele were patients from the elite and upper classes.

Now a successful doctor, he becomes disturbed by a letter from his daughter, stating her intention to marry an American instructor who helped her to study in the United States. Yet still Yi's greed and ambition persist, as he presents a Koryŏ inlaid cela-

이면서 학자이기도 한 전광용의 단편소설에서 자주 사용되는 소설 미학이기도 하다. 여기에서 "목숨을 걸고 삶의 도피행을 같이한 유일물이요 어찌보면 인생의 반려이기도 한" 회중시계는 독자로 하여금 주인공 이인국의 파란만장한 과거의 삶을 엿볼 수 있게 하는 서사적 장치로서 기능하고 있다. 현재—과거—현재로 이어지는 역전적 시간 구성을 취하고 있는 이 소설에서 과거로의 여행을 가능케 하는 것이 바로 '월섬 17석(Waltham 17 Jewels)'의 회중시계이기 때문이다. 제국대학 졸업 시에 받은 선물이라는 점에서 명예의 상징이지만, 자신의 영욕을 함께한 산 증인이라는 점에서 이 회중시계의 상징적인 의미는 양가적이다.

그동안 문학사에서는 이 작품을 '교활한 기회주의자' 혹은 '과잉 적응주의자'인 이인국이라는 인물을 비난, 조소하고 있는 풍자적인 작품으로서 평가해 왔다. 그러나 오랫동안 문학사적 평가의 기준으로 작용했던 민족주의의 압도적 영향력 때문인지 이 작품에서 주인공의 간혹 내비치는 인생에 대한 근원적인 공허감과 상실감이라는 파토스는 그다지 주목을 받지 못한 면이 있다. 비록 그의 삶은 외형적으로는 매우 화려한 듯이 보이지

don vase to an employee at the American Embassy in order to obtain an invitation from the U.S. Department of State, so he can travel to the United States to meet his daughter.

The story "Kapitan Ri" actually begins with Yi Inguk checking his watch for an appointment at the American Embassy, then shifts to his memories of the past, and ends with him heading to Bando Hotel after giving a Koryŏ inlaid celadon vase as a gift to the embassy employee. Such an inverted narrative structure was often used by Chŏn, who was both a writer and a scholar. Here, the pocket watch, which is the "only remaining object that had escaped with him...and, in a sense, his life's companion," is a narrative device that opens up to the reader Yi's tumultuous past. In fact, it is this "Waltham 17 Jewel" pocket watch that makes the journey into the past possible. The watch is an ambivalent object: both a symbol of honor, since Yi received it at the time of his graduation from the Imperial University, and a witness to Yi's life, his glory, and shame.

Throughout the history of Korean literature, this story has been seen as a work that criticizes and ridicules its protagonist, Yi Inguk, who has been la-

만, 해방 직후의 혼란 속에서 아내를 잃어야 했고, 자신이 등떠밀어 소련으로 유학을 보낸 아들의 소식은 알 길이 없는 상황 속에서, 미국에 간 딸마저 자신의 기대에서 벗어나 '국제결혼'을 선언함으로써, '꺼삐딴 리'의 내면은 실상 공허하기 이를 데 없다. 딸의 결혼 소식에 심란한 마음을 '미국 혼반'이라며 위무하면서 그가 내뱉은 "자위인지 체념인지 모를 푸념"은 이제는 그의 곁에 없는 가족에게 "죄를 지은 것과 같은" 무의식이 낳은 히스테리적 반응에 다름아닌 것이다. 또한 소설의 시작과 끝 부분에서 그가 미 국무성의 초청장에 연연하는 모습은 자신의 과거에 드리워진 '그늘'을 감춤으로써 현재를 정당화하려는 '확증 편향(confirmation bias)'의 공허한 몸부림으로 느껴진다. 이런 점에서 "그들이 그렇게 하지 않을 수 없었던 필연성이 우리 민족이 겪은 역경과 비극이 치른 것의 거스름돈"이라 했던 한 원로 시인의 언급은 「꺼삐딴 리」를 오늘날의 관점에서 새롭게 해석하기 위해 되새겨 볼 필요가 있다.

beled a "sly opportunist" and an "excessive adaptor." However, possibly due to the overwhelming influence of democracy, which has long stood as the standard for literary evaluation, Yi's pathos—a sense of emptiness and loss—that he expresses about life occasionally in the story has not received much attention. Although his life seemed glamorous on the outside, "Kapitan Ri" was empty inside. Not only did he lose his wife in the chaos that came immediately after liberation, but he also had no idea whether his son, whom he sent to Russia for studies, was living or dead. On top of this, his daughter, who went to the United States, has declared that she will marry an American against his wishes.

At the news of his daughter's marriage, though, he thinks it might not be such a bad idea to get "started early as a member of an American family." These words, spoken as a consolation or in resignation, are, in fact, a hysteric response of his subconscious "feeling of having sinned" against his family, who are no longer with him. Also, his fixation on receiving an invitation from the U.S. Department of State in the beginning and end of the story feels like an empty struggle for "confirmation bias," which attempts to justify the present by hiding the "shade" of his past. In this regard, if we re-examine and revisit "Kapitan Ri" from our perspective, it is necessary for us to reflect on the words of an elderly poet, who said: "the inevitability of their acts can be seen as remnants of the hardships and tragedy the people of our country experienced."

비평의 목소리

Critical Acclaim

그는 우선 '식민지의 백성'이었다. 그러나 그 식민지의 백성이 지배 국가의 제국대학에서 '시계'를 탈 때부터 동족에 대한 선민의식을 가지게 되고 동시에 그 의식은 지배자에 대한 노예의식으로 변하게 되는 것이다. 주인에게 반항할 줄 모르는 노예는 '내일'을 거부하고 다만 그날그날의 안락만을 추구하는 것이다. 그날그날의 안락을 보증받기 위해서는 지배자의 명령에 복종하는 습성과 함께, 사사건건이 그 지배자를 이용할 수 있는 찬스를 노리는 기회주의자가 되지 않으면 안 된다. 그는 그 습성과 기회주의가 철저하면 할수록 오히려 지배자 권 내에 들어간 것 같은 착각에 사로잡힌다. 이것이 그

He was the "citizen of a colony." Yet from the time he receives a watch from the Imperial University, he develops a sense of elitism against people of the same race, and that elitism transforms into servitude for the ruling people. A slave who doesn't know to oppose the master only refuses to accept "tomorrow" and pursues comfort day to day. To ensure his daily comfort, he not only has to obey the master but also to become an opportunist who is always on the lookout for a chance to manipulate the master for personal gain. The more thorough such habits and opportunism become, the more he becomes deluded that he can influence the master.

의 정신구조의 단면이다. (……) 필자는 이인국 박사의 인간상은 우리나라 근대화 과정이 어쩔 수 없이 빚어낸 슬픈 인간 유형의 축도라고 했다. 이인국적 인간형의 비열과 위선과 죄악이 아무리 미운 것일지라도, 그들이 그렇게 하지 않을 수 없었던 필연성이 우리 민족이 겪은 역경과 비극이 치른 것의 거스름돈이라고 한다면, 그들의 그 비열과 위선과 죄악은 결코 이인국 박사 개인의 책임만은 아니다! 전광용의 이 작품이 우리에게 어필하는 것은 바로 이 점이 아닐까. 그러나 우리는 그의 그들 세대에 대한 고발 정신에 더 한층 비중을 주어야 할 것이다.

천상병, 「근대적 인간 유형의 축도-「꺼삐딴 리」」,

『현대한국문학전집』 5권, 신구문화사, 1972

이 소설의 맨 앞부분은 주인공 이인국 박사가 미국 대사관 직원 브라운과의 약속이 20분밖에 안 남은 것을 확인하는 것으로 꾸며져 있으며 끝부분은 이인국 박사가 브라운을 만나 선물을 주고 나와서는 반도호텔로 가는 것으로 처리되어 있다. 그럼 이 작품의 중간부분은 어떤 내용으로 채워져 있는가. 맨 앞부분과 뒷부분을

This is one side of the protagonist's cognitive structure... I believe that the image of Dr. Yi Inguk is a miniature copy of mournful people who have been shaped in the process of modernization in Korea. No matter how detestable the baseness, hypocrisy, and sins committed by people like Yi Inguk, the inevitability of their acts can be seen as remnants of the hardships and tragedy the Korean people experienced. Therefore, they are not solely responsible for their own sins! This is the reason this short story by Chŏn Kwangyong appeals to us. Yet we must also give greater due to the efforts of their generation to expose the dark side of modernization.

Cheon Sang-byeong, "Scaled Models of Modern Human Types—'Kapitan Ri,'" *Complete Collection of Modern Korean Literature*, Vol. 5 (Seoul: Singu Munhwasa, 1972)

In the very beginning of this story, the protagonist Dr. Yi Inguk is waiting for his appointment with Mr. Brown at the American Embassy, 20 minutes before the meeting. It ends with Dr. Yi giving Brown a gift and heading to Bando Hotel. So what does the body of this story contain? The reader learns about the life of Dr. Yi, who lived from the

제외한 나머지 중간부분에서 독자들은 일제 때부터 해방기를 거쳐 50년대에 이르기까지 이인국 박사가 과잉적응주의, 에고이즘, 출세제일주의의 방식으로 살아온 과정을 들을 수 있게 된다. 이인국 박사가 딸 나미가 미국인과 국제결혼한다는 사실에 가벼운 분노를 느끼면서도 자신의 경력에 윤기를 더할 셈으로 도미할 계획을 세우는 것을 '현재'라고 본다면, 「꺼삐딴 리」에서의 '현재'는 더럽고도 탐욕스럽게 살아온 '과거'에 붙어 있는 꼬리에 지나지 않는다. '과거'를 보면 이인국 박사의 '현재' 이후의 삶의 방식은 불문가지다. 「꺼삐딴 리」의 경우, '현재'는 '과거'의 확인 행위에 지나지 않으며 동시에 추인하는 것에 불과하다.

조남현, 「리얼리티에의 투망, 그 정신과 방법」, 《문학사상》, 1988

소설 「꺼삐딴 리」에서 주목되는 것은 작품의 서술구조와 연관되는 문제이다. 이 소설은 행위의 인과적 연결이나 기억의 단편이나 생각들이 얽혀 과거의 시간과 현재의 시간이 교차된다. 이야기의 전개를 위해 행위의 논리적 일관성을 유도하지 않고, 오히려 인물의 성격을 특징짓는 삽화들을 덧붙일 뿐이다. 그러므로 이 작품에

Japanese Colonial Era through the Liberation and into the 1950s, excessively adapting to political and social changes, and immersed in egoism and careerism. In the "present," Dr. Yi feels a bit angry at the fact that his daughter Nami will be marrying an American, yet he plans to add luster to his career through this marriage. But the "present" in "Kapitan Ri" is only a tail attached to his "past," when he led a dirty and greedy life. When we look at the "past," we can clearly infer the way he will lead his life after the present. In the case of "Kapitan Ri," the "present" is nothing more than a verification and confirmation of the past.

Cho Nam-hyeon, "Casting the Net on the Reality, its Essence
and Methods," Munhak Sasang, September 1988.

A noteworthy element in the short story "Kapitan Ri" is related to its narrative structure. The past and the present intersect through causal connections of actions and entangled fragments of memories and thoughts. Instead of inducing a logical consistency of actions, for the progress of the plot, the author only inserts and adds anecdotes that signify the personalities of characters. That is why it is difficult to distinguish the different stages of the plot, and

서는 플롯의 단계를 구분하기 어렵고, 갈등의 고조 상태나 그 파국 등을 찾아볼 수 없다. 현실의 행위 속에 과거의 기억들이 끼어들고 있어서 사건이 시간적 순서를 잃고 있다. 이것은 행위의 연결보다는 인물의 성격화에 주력하기 위해 고안된 구성 방법이라고 할 수 있는데, 구조적 완결성을 목표로 하는 단편 형식의 이완을 피할 수 없게 하고 있다. 결국 이 소설은 구성의 요건을 희생시키면서 인간성의 내면과 그 변모과정을 추적하고 있는 특이한 작품이라고 할 것이다.

권영민, 「전광용의 현실인식과 소설적 기법」,

『전광용대표작선집』, 책세상, 1994

neither the escalation of conflicts nor the results appear in this story. Memories of the past interfere in the actions of the present, and, as a result, events lose their chronological order. We can say that this method has been developed to focus more on the characters than on the connections between actions. Through this method, the text cannot avoid relaxing the structure of the short story, for which structural tightness is essential. In the end, this story succeeds in tracing the inner world of a person and their changes by sacrificing the elements of composition.

Kwon Young-min, "Chǒn Kwangyong's Awareness of the Reality and Fiction Technique," *Collection of Major Works by Chǒn Kwangyong*, (Seoul: Ch'aeksesang, 1994)

전광용

백사(白史) 전광용은 1919년(실제 생일은 음력 1918년 9월 5일이라고 함) 함경남도 북청에서 태어났다. 과수원을 운영하는 평범한 농가의 2남 4녀 중 장남으로 태어난 그는 고향의 북청공업농립학교를 졸업한 뒤 해방 직전인 1945년 봄 경성경제전문학교에 진학하였다. 해방 후 '국립서울대학교설립에 관한 법령'(이른바 '국대안')에 의해 경성경제전문학교가 서울대학교 상과대학으로 바뀌는 과정에서 문학에 뜻을 두고 서울대학교 문리과대학 국어국문학과에 입학하면서 진로를 바꾸게 된다.

1939년《동아일보》신춘문예 동화 부분에 「별나라 공주와 토끼」가 당선된 이력이 있는 그는 1948년 정한숙, 정한모 등과《주막》동인을 결성하면서 본격적인 창작 활동을 시작한다. 1955년《조선일보》신춘문예에 「흑산도」가 당선되면서 늦깎이로 문단에 등단한 이후 「꺼삐딴 리」「충매화」「목단강행열차」 등 30여 편의 단편과 『태백산맥』『나신』 등 4편의 장편소설을 발표하였다. 작품집으로는 『흑산도』(1959), 『꺼삐딴 리』(1975), 『동혈인

Chŏn Kwangyong

Baeksa Chŏn Kwangyong was born in 1919 in Bukch'ŏng, South Hamgyŏng Province (His actual birth date is September 5, 1918, by the lunar calendar). The eldest son of six children, whose parents ran an orchard, he graduate from Bukch'ŏng Agricultural School and entered Kyŏngsŏng Business College in spring 1945, immediately prior to the liberation of Korea from Japanese rule. Yet after the liberation, when Kyŏngsŏng Business College became the College of Commerce at Seoul National University, according to the Act related to the Establishment of Seoul National University, or "kukdaean" for short, Chŏn changed his career to studying in the Korean Language and Literature Department at the Seoul National University College of Liberal Arts and Sciences.

After making his literary debut by winning the children's story award in the *Donga Ilbo* Spring Literary Contest in 1939 with "Byŏlnara gongju and t'okki," Chŏn began his creative literary career with Chung Hansook and Jung Hanmo, forming a literary cote-

간』(1977), 『목단강행열차』(1978)가 있고, 사후 23년 만인 2011년 『전광용문학전집』(전 6권)이 간행되었다. 전광용의 작품은 대부분 인간의 삶과 현실에 대한 진실 탐구에 목표를 두었고 엄격한 윤리적 가치관을 통해 주제를 표출하면서 현실 비판을 드러내고 있는 것이 특징이다. 만년에는 월남민으로서 망향의 정을 그린 작품을 창작하기도 했다.

소설가로 등단하던 1955년 모교인 서울대학교 국어국문학과에 교수로 부임한 그는 30여 년간 재직하면서 교육과 연구 양면에서 학자로서도 활발한 활동을 펼쳤다. 국어국문학과에 현대문학 전공과정을 처음으로 개설하여 후진을 양성하는 한편으로 개화기 신소설 연구에 선편을 쥐면서 현대문학 연구의 학문적 기초를 쌓은 것으로 평가받고 있다. 동인문학상, 대한민국문학상, 사상계 논문상 등을 수상하였다.

rie named "Chumak." In 1955, he won the *Chosŏn Ilbo* Spring Literary Contest with "Hŭksando," and since then he has published about 30 short stories, including "Kapitan Ri," "Chungmaehwa," "Mokdanganghaeng yŏlcha (Train to Mudanjiang)," and four full-length novels, including *Taebaek sanmaek* (The Taebaek Mountains) and *Nasin* (Nude). His collections of short stories include *Hŭksando* (1959), *Kapitan Ri* (1975), *Donghyŏl in'gan* (1977), and *Mokdanganghaeng yŏlcha* (1978). In 2011, 23 years after his death, six volumes of the *Complete Works of Chŏn Kwangyong* were published. Most of his works focus on investigating the truth in human lives and reality, and he criticized reality by expressing the theme of the story through a strict moral value system. Toward the end of his life, Chon wrote about the homesickness he felt as a defector to South Korea.

In 1955, the year he made his debut as a novelist, he began his post as a professor of Korean Language and Literature at Seoul National University. For the next 30 years, he was actively involved in education and research as a scholar. For the first time, he launched the Modern Literature Program in the Korean Language and Literature Department to foster future scholars; at the same time, he was acclaimed for his efforts in establishing the academic basis for the study of Modern Korean Literature, as he led the research of *sinsosŏl* (new fiction) from the Enlightenment period. He has also been the recipient of many awards, including the Dongin Literary Award, the Korea Literary Award, and the *Sasanggye* Academic Paper Award.

번역 **마샬 필** Translated by Marshall R. Pihl

마샬 필은 1957년 서울에 주둔하고 있던 한국 군사고문단의 공보장교로 배치되었을 때 처음으로 한국을 접했다. 1960년 하버드대학교를 졸업하고 월간지인 《사상계》의 연구부에 합류하기 위해서 한국에 갔고, 사상계사에서 잡지사의 직원들의 후견 아래 논문과 사설 등을 영역했다. 2년 후 서울대학교에 입학해 한국어와 문학을 공부했고, 1965년 서울대학교에서 석사 학위를 받은 최초의 서양인이 되었다. 이어서 한국의 구전서사인 판소리에 관한 논문으로 하버드대학교에서 박사 학위를 받았다. 한국 현대문학 최초의 영문 선집 《한국에 귀 기울이기》(1973)를 편집했고 오영수의 단편집인 《착한 사람들》(1986)을 번역했으며 한국소설 선집 《유형의 땅: 현대 한국 소설》(1993)을 공역했다. 그 외에도 1994년 하버드대학교에서 그가 쓴 최초의 영문 판소리 연구서 《한국 민담 가수》가 나왔다. 하버드대학교에서 한국문학 전임강사와 여름학교 학장을 지낸 뒤 1995년 사망시까지 하와이대학교에서 한국문학을 가르쳤다.

Marshall R. Pihl saw Korea for the first time as a soldier in 1957, when he was assigned to the Public Information Office of the Korean Military Advisory Group in Seoul. Upon graduation from Harvard College in 1960, he returned to join the research department of the monthly journal *World of Thought* (Sasanggye), where he translated articles and editorials into English under the tutelage of the magazine's staff. Two years later, he entered Seoul National University to study Korean language and literature, emerging in 1965 as the first Westerner to have earned a master's degree there. Subsequent study led to the Harvard Ph.D. for a dissertation on the Korean oral narrative *p'ansori*. He edited one of the first English-language anthologies of contemporary Korean literature, *Listening to Korea* (Praeger, 1973); translated a collection of stories by Oh Young-su, *The Good People* (Heinemann Asia, 1986), co-translated the anthology *Land of Exile: Contemporary Korean Fiction* (M.E. Sharpe, 1993); and wrote the first English-language study of *p'ansori, The Korean Singer of Tales* (Harvard University Press, 1994). After serving as a Senior Lecturer on Korean Literature and Director of the Summer School at Harvard, he taught Korean Literature at the University of Hawai'i until his passing in 1995.

감수 **브루스 풀턴** Edited by Bruce Fulton

브루스 풀턴은 한국문학 작품을 다수 영역해서 영미권에 소개하고 있다. 『별사-한국 여성 소설가 단편집』『순례자의 노래-한국 여성의 새로운 글쓰기』『유형의 땅』(공역, Marshall R. Pihl)을 번역하였다. 가장 최근 번역한 작품으로는 오정희의 소설집 『불의 강 외 단편소설 선집』, 조정래의 장편소설 『오 하느님』이 있다. 브루스 풀턴은 『레디메이드 인생』(공역, 김종운), 『현대 한국 소설 선집』(공편, 권영민), 『촛농 날개-악타 코리아나 한국 단편 선집』 외 다수의 작품의 번역과 편집을 담당했다. 브루스 풀턴은 서울대학교 국어국문학과에서 박사 학위를 받고 캐나다의 브리티시컬럼비아 대학 민영빈 한국문학 기금 교수로 재직하고 있다. 다수의 번역문학기금과 번역문학상 등을 수상한 바 있다.

Bruce Fulton is the translator of numerous volumes of modern Korean fiction, including the award-winning women's anthologies *Words of Farewell: Stories by Korean Women Writers (Seal Press, 1989) and Wayfarer: New Writing by Korean Women* (Women in Translation, 1997), and, with Marshall R. Pihl, *Land of Exile: Contemporary Korean Fiction*, rev. and exp. ed. (M.E. Sharpe, 2007). Their most recent translations are *River of Fire and Other Stories* by O Chŏng-hŭi (Columbia University Press, 2012), and *How in Heaven's Name: A Novel of World War II* by Cho Chŏngnae (MerwinAsia, 2012). Bruce Fulton is co-translator (with Kim Chong-un) of *A Ready-Made Life: Early Masters of Modern Korean Fiction* (University of Hawai'i Press, 1998), co-editor (with Kwon Young-min) of *Modern Korean Fiction: An Anthology* (Columbia University Press, 2005), and editor of *Waxen Wings: The* Acta Koreana *Anthology of Short Fiction From Korea* (Koryo Press, 2011). The Fultons have received several awards and fellowships for their translations, including a National Endowment for the Arts Translation Fellowship, the first ever given for a translation from the Korean, and a residency at the Banff International Literary Translation Centre, the first ever awarded for translators from any Asian language. Bruce Fulton is the inaugural holder of the Young-Bin Min Chair in Korean Literature and Literary Translation, Department of Asian Studies, University of British Columbia.

바이링궐 에디션 한국 대표 소설 105
꺼삐딴 리

2015년 1월 9일 초판 1쇄 발행

지은이 전광용 | 옮긴이 마샬 필 | 펴낸이 김재범
감수 브루스 풀턴 | 기획위원 정은경, 전성태, 이경재
편집 정수인, 이은혜, 김형욱, 윤단비 | 관리 박신영
펴낸곳 (주)아시아 | 출판등록 2006년 1월 27일 제406-2006-000004호
주소 서울특별시 동작구 서달로 161-1(흑석동 100-16)
전화 02.821.5055 | 팩스 02.821.5057 | 홈페이지 www.bookasia.org
ISBN 979-11-5662-067-9 (set) | 979-11-5662-082-2 (04810)
값은 뒤표지에 있습니다.

Bi-lingual Edition Modern Korean Literature 105
Kapitan Ri

Written by Chŏn Kwangyong | Translated by Marshall R. Pihl
Published by Asia Publishers | 161-1, Seodal-ro, Dongjak-gu, Seoul, Korea
Homepage Address www.bookasia.org | Tel. (822).821.5055 | Fax. (822).821.5057
First published in Korea by Asia Publishers 2015
ISBN 979-11-5662-067-9 (set) | 979-11-5662-082-2 (04810)

.